THE ODDEST LITTLE FLOWER SHOP

A sweet, uplifting romance

Beth Good

Thimblerig Books

Copyright © 2023 Beth Good

All rights reserved. Beth Good has asserted her right under Section 77 of the Copyright, Designs and Patents Act 1988 to be identified as the author of this work.

No part of this book can be reproduced in part or in whole or transferred by any means without the express written permission of the author. This is a work of fiction. Any names of places or characters are the products of the author's imagination. Any resemblance to actual events, places or persons, living or dead, is entirely coincidental.

ISBN: 9798853276796
Imprint: Independently published

CHAPTER ONE

Thirteen months since she'd walked out of the door, rucksack on her back, Penny walked back in, dumped her rucksack in the hall and called out, 'Dad? Sylvia? I'm home.'

Silence greeted her.

'Dad? Sylvia? Is *anybody* here? Nobody? Seriously?' Penny blew out a gusty sigh and shook her head before carrying her rucksack up to her bedroom at the back of the modest semi-detached in Milton Keynes.

She'd been backpacking all over the world, travelling and sight-seeing, and had seen some astonishing things and met the most *amazing* people along the way. Places she would always hold in her heart, people she would never forget. Having been gone over a year, she'd told her dad she would be back this afternoon, arriving on the train from London. Which had been on time.

Yet he hadn't bothered to pick her up from the station. Or warned her that he wouldn't be turning up.

Still, that was her dad all over, she thought with a rueful shrug. Her father would never change, so there was little point hoping for it.

She stopped dead on the threshold to her bedroom, staring inside. Things had been changed around in her absence. Not surprising, given the length of time she had been away. But she'd warned them she'd be home today, and she thought that either Dad or her stepmum Sylvia might have taken five minutes to shift the packing boxes off the bare mattress and find a fresh sheet for her. Too much to hope for, like being picked up from the station, perhaps.

Still, the walk from the station had been refreshing, and the sunny weather was a treat after three weeks of non-stop rain in Sri Lanka. And it would only take her a few minutes to stack the boxes in the corner and reclaim her bed with some fresh linen from the airing cupboard.

Her stepmother didn't have a job these days, having 'damaged' her back doing aerobics, but from what Dad had said during Penny's monthly calls home, Sylvia was still always busy, meeting friends for lunch or helping out at the local beauty salon, moonlighting as a manicurist without telling the benefits office. These were tough times, after all. Her dad worked in trucking logistics, which basically meant telling which trucks where to go and when, and what they would be carrying. It was a big company and his job could be very stressful at times. Which no doubt was why he hadn't been able to meet her off the train this afternoon. All the same, she felt a pique of hurt.

Gingerly, Penny heaved the heavy boxes off her bed and into a corner, stacking them one on top of the other. The boxes were all sealed, so she had no way of knowing what was inside, but they were all marked with Sylvia's name and weighed a ton.

Afterwards she was sweating and dishevelled, and had to throw open her bedroom window to get cool air on her face. She had done a few jobs abroad that required shifting heavy boxes, and not thought much about it at the time, but she hadn't expected to be doing it straight after returning home from her year abroad.

Again, that pique of hurt.

'Oh, for goodness sake...' She stopped such thoughts in their tracks, shaking her head. 'Yes, your room's been used for storage. So what? Get over it, Penny. You're twenty-three, not three.' She had spoken the words out loud, pointing an accusatory finger at herself in her bedroom mirror. But she jumped on seeing her stepmother's heavily made-up face glowering at her from the doorway, and spun, saying hurriedly, 'Sylvia! I didn't hear you come in.'

'Obviously,' Sylvia said with a dry intonation. Long hair piled on top of her head in a chignon, dyed an unlikely pineapple-blonde, her stepmum was clad in a skin-tight leopard skin skirt with a sleeveless fitted blouse. 'Been messing about with my barbells, have you?'

'Your *what*?'

'Didn't your dad tell you?' Sylvia flexed her biceps, which were certainly very muscular. 'I'm selling free weights now as a side-hustle.'

'No,' Penny said, wiping the sweat from her brow and trying not to roll her eyes. 'He must have, um, forgotten.' She frowned. 'Wait... Barbells? I thought you had a bad back?'

Ignoring that observation, Sylvia looked her stepdaughter up and down, scarlet lips pursed as though sucking on a lemon. 'You look like you've been dragged through a hedge backwards, my girl. And those clothes... I can smell them from here. You'd best take a shower and change into something more respectable before your dad comes home. He's due back any minute.'

'Sorry,' Penny said, acutely embarrassed and not a little upset by this unpleasant welcome after more than a year away. 'I've been travelling for days. I guess I probably look a bit grubby. But it's hard to wash your clothes and get a shower while on the road.' Penny could see that Sylvia was unimpressed with this lame explanation, so gave up. 'I'll sort myself out, you're right. Give me ten minutes.' She paused, adding awkwardly, 'It's good to be back.'

Sylvia said nothing to this but turned on her heel and headed back down to the kitchen, where Penny could now hear the kettle beginning to boil.

Home sweet home, she thought grimly. But with no money left and no immediate job prospects, she wasn't in a position to move out. Indeed, lumping and liking it seemed to be high on her agenda instead.

With an exploratory sniff of her armpits, Penny began dragging crumpled possessions out of her rucksack.

It was definitely time to freshen up!

Her father did at least hug her when they were reunited. Thankfully, she'd showered and changed into her last clean outfit by then, so he didn't wrinkle his nose at the same time. He looked older but was still her lovely dad, with sideburns and a whiskery beard. 'You've lost weight,' he told her critically, holding her out at arms' length to examine her. 'Didn't you eat properly in those foreign places? All that funny food, I suppose. Not that I blame you... I probably wouldn't have eaten much either.'

Grinning at his expression, Penny shook her head. 'I've just been doing lots of exercise. Walking long distances, physically demanding jobs, that's all. I needed to lose a bit of baby fat anyway. It's great to be back, Dad. And you're looking well too.'

She paused, glancing sideways at Sylvia, who was dishing out dinner. Sausages and mash with boiled cabbage and gravy. Traditional British fare, and usually Penny would have loved it. It was just she'd grown more accustomed to spicy foods while she was away. But she would soon adjust back to English eating habits, she told herself.

'Sylvia's looking good too,' she added, forcing herself to be friendly. 'You're doing your hair a new way, aren't you?'

Sylvia flashed her a look that reminded Penny of a particularly menacing Rottweiler she'd encountered on her travels.

'No.'

'Sorry, my mistake. Well, it looks very nice anyway.' Penny glanced at her dad for support. But he shook his head and drew her to the dinner table. She whispered under her breath, 'Have I done something wrong? Sylvia doesn't seem pleased to see me again.'

Her father scratched his head. 'Oh, don't mind Syl. Her back's hurting again, I expect. Plus, she's always a bit moody these days. She's at *that age*, you know.'

'What age?' Penny frowned.

'*Men-o-pause*,' he mouthed, glancing cautiously over his shoulder, as though afraid Sylvia might suddenly burst out of the kitchen, greasy frying pan in hand, ready to clock him one.

'Oh, right.' Unsure that menopause alone could explain Sylvia's charm deficiency, Penny shrugged nonetheless. 'That's sad... I'm sorry to hear that.' She was making it sound like someone had died, she realised. But maybe they had. The old friendly Sylvia had been murdered and this grim-faced new Sylvia had taken her place. It would make an interesting twist on the B-movie premise, she considered, swiftly disguising her snort of laughter as a cough.

Invasion of the Stepmother Snatchers.

'Try not to speak to her, you'll be fine.' Her dad hesitated. 'Try not to be at home much either. I find staying out and not speaking seems to work.'

Penny dug her hands into the pockets of her long shorts and said nothing. It seemed wisest. And it was none of her business. But it struck her that Dad and Sylvia were going through a rocky patch in their marriage.

Her dad ambled to the sideboard, poured himself a large whisky, and then removed a wodge of envelopes from a drawer. 'These came for you while you were away, love. A year's worth of post... Not much, I suppose, for all those months you were away.' He sipped his whisky with the restrained air of a man more accustomed to swigging it generously when nobody was looking. 'I hope there wasn't anything urgent in there.'

'I hope so too.' Penny weighed the stack of envelopes in her hand, feeling disheartened. She would have to trawl through them for anything urgent, and the sooner the better. 'I let my bank and the taxman know that I would be abroad, and thought I'd sorted everything else before I left the country. Perhaps most of this is junk mail.' But some of the envelopes looked scarily official.

After dinner, she threw herself into an armchair, legs dangling over the arm, and sorted through the letters while watching a TV soap with her dad and Sylvia.

The other two seemed enraptured with the soap opera, which she could hardly follow, having never watched it before. There were so many characters, and all their lives seemed hopelessly entangled... But she smiled whenever Dad and Sylvia smiled and laughed dutifully when they laughed, feeling it was important to fit back into family life now that she had returned to Milton Keynes. Though she hoped that she would soon be busy with a new job.

One of the envelopes was a letter to do with her redundancy. She had been made redundant about three months before she left on her travels. In fact, that was why she had left to go abroad. She had received a large severance package along with five of her co-workers at the estate agents where she'd been working for nearly a year. The company had been streamlining, apparently, and she was streamlined right out of a job.

She had never gone aboard after university, heading straight into her job as an estate agent after finishing her studies. Being made redundant had been her opportunity to see the world, and she had seized on it enthusiastically. Of course, the money had not taken her the whole way around the globe. Once her petty cash ran out, she had been forced to take casual employment along the way, washing dishes or helping out at funfairs and other tourist venues, basically working her bed and board from one country to another.

She had made dozens of wonderful new friends who had no doubt forgotten her as soon as she'd moved on, and taken thousands of photos and videos, all safely stored now in the cloud.

It had been the trip of a lifetime and she didn't regret a minute of it. But now she was home and utterly broke.

She needed a new job, that was clear.

Putting aside the letter connected to her redundancy, which contained nothing of special interest, she turned to one of the last letters in the stack. It was a brown envelope, large and oblong, and struck her as being a little fussy in its presentation, with her name and address typed and visible through a see-through plastic window. She tore it open and, while her dad and Sylvia continued to exclaim over the antics of the soap opera they were watching, read its contents with open-mouthed astonishment.

'Good God!'

'I know,' her dad agreed, knocking back his whisky. 'Who would have thought it, eh? Bertha turning out to be a man, I mean.' Then, studying her face, he must have realised she hadn't been exclaiming at the convoluted soap storyline and reached for the remote instead to pause the television. 'What's up, Penny, love? You're looking a bit pasty. Don't tell me that's a big bill.' He was looking worried too, perhaps fearing he would have to lend her the money to pay any outstanding bills. For he knew she had zero money left.

'No, nothing like that.' Swallowing hard, Penny passed him the solicitor's letter she had received. 'Apparently, up until last year, I had a grandmother still living. Her name was Cecily.' She bit her lip, watching his face as he scanned the letter. 'Did you know about her? I thought you said my grandparents were dead on both sides of the family.

Long dead, you told me.' She was feeling stunned and a little bewildered. 'But that letter says my grandmother died *last year,* and that she left me a property in Cornwall. A small shop, it says, with a one-bedroom flat above.'

Her father's eyes were fairly bulging as he read the letter through twice, showed it to a clearly curious and impatient Sylvia, and then handed it back to Penny. 'Honestly, I had no idea your mum's mother was still alive. I didn't try to hide it from you. I genuinely wasn't aware of her existence. I'm so sorry, love. All these years and you could have got to know her... That's awful.' He was looking contrite. 'But she's left you something in her Will. What a turn-up, eh? Of course, there will be quite a bit of paperwork involved. But it'll be worth *something*.'

'Yes, I'll have to sell it, agreed. I don't know the first thing about running a shop. The solicitor says it's a flower shop too. I know nothing about flowers. It's true I did a two-week stint picking tulips near Amsterdam. But I don't think that qualifies me to be a florist.' Penny's heart was beating fast though. She had been worrying about money, and now surely her prayers had been answered. 'It says in the letter Cecily had been in a care home for a while before she died, poor thing. That's heartbreaking. To think I could have visited her...'

Her father shrugged, pulling a face. 'Your mum never mentioned that her mother was still alive, I'm sure of it. I'm sorry.'

Penny believed him. Her mum had been very

secretive about her past, for reasons best known to herself. 'That's okay, Dad. Too late to do anything about it now, anyway. But I expect that means the shop has been standing empty a long time. It's probably not in good condition. But it's in Cornwall. Property is fairly expensive in the south-west, isn't it? I expect I could sell it easily.'

'Or you could run it yourself as a going concern,' Sylvia said flatly. She crossed her legs and folded her arms, looking back at the television. No doubt she was wishing that Penny's dad would turn it back on so she could finish watching her favourite show. 'Cornwall's nice. I went there on holiday once. You could settle down there. Make a life for yourself.'

Penny was astonished by this intervention, but she reddened, understanding only too well. Sylvia was not happy that she had come home again, disturbing her peaceful way of life, and this inheritance of a shop far away was a godsend. The perfect opportunity to get rid of her annoying stepdaughter.

'First thing to do is get in touch with these solicitors,' Penny pointed out in a practical way, folding up the letter and sliding it back into its official-looking envelope. 'That letter was dated eight months ago, and they've had no reply, so perhaps it's been sold or bequeathed to someone else by now. I don't know how these things work. But I'll give the solicitors' firm a call tomorrow and find out for sure.'

Sylvia reached for the remote and put the program

back on without further comment. Penny's dad gave her a thumbs-up along with a reassuring smile before going back to watching the program.

Penny tried to enjoy the bizarre antics of the soap characters, but her head was in a totally different place now. Lying on the golden sand of a Cornish beach with the deep-blue rollers of the Atlantic Ocean thundering towards her and hunky surfers balancing on boards far out among the waves…

It seemed her life was about to take a brand-new turn instead of reaching the dead-end she'd expected. It was an amazing prospect and she could hardly wait to find out where it would lead her.

CHAPTER TWO

'Erm, that's not the way to the bathroom, Franklin,' Gideon interjected, linking his arm with his godfather's and guiding him patiently towards the men's toilets in the care home. He helped him inside, did the necessary, and then aided the elderly man with washing his hands.

Outside, he found one of the nurses waiting for them.

Jeremy beamed at him, taking Franklin's other arm. The nurse's salt-and-pepper hair stuck up like the bristles of a brush and he wore one elaborate earring that jingled. 'I would have done that, Gideon,' he said with a wink. 'There was no need.'

'It was no trouble.' Gently, Gideon patted his godfather on the back and said loudly, for the old man's hearing was no longer what it had been, 'I'm off now, Franklin. I'm glad we got to walk about the garden today. Such lovely weather... I'll see you again the day after tomorrow. You look after yourself, alright?'

'Eh?' Franklin was blinking at him, his eyes slightly glazed. His eyesight was no longer what it had been either. 'What's that you say?' he mumbled.

'I said, I'll be back before you know it.' Gideon paused, regarding him steadily. But his godfather seemed to be staring dimly ahead now, lost in the past or some such reverie. His hair was thinning, showing his scalp, and his narrow torso was wrapped in a high-necked sweater despite the summer heat, for he was having trouble regulating his body temperature these days. 'It's Gideon, your godson,' he added softly, feeling a painful tug of wistfulness as he recalled the strong, intelligent man who had taken him fishing and read books to him as a kid, and taught him so many things over the years since then.

Franklin blinked again, looking around at him with slow dignity. 'I know who you are. I'm not in my dotage, you know. I'll see you next time. But now, it's time for my bath.' He pointed shakily at the hall clock, which was showing just after half-past four. 'You know I like to take a bath before teatime. If they'll let me... They're always saying I take too long and my meal gets cold.'

Gideon glanced at Jeremy, who shrugged and laughed.

'Bath-time it is,' the nurse agreed cheerily as they parted in the corridor. 'He's sharp for ninety-three.'

'Don't I know it,' Gideon threw back at him, waving to both as he strode towards the care home entrance.

Although it was quite late in the afternoon, it was

summer and the sparkling Cornish sun was warm on Gideon's back as he made his way down the high street, back towards the ivy-covered house he'd shared with his godfather for the past five years, since moving back from London.

He hadn't ever wanted Franklin to move out of the home he'd inherited from his parents. But the old man had no living relatives left and had been getting lonely during the daytime, for Gideon worked full-time, including some evening shifts, and couldn't always be there if his godfather got into trouble, which was quite frequently now that his dementia had worsened.

The formal diagnosis of dementia had come five years ago.

For a long time afterwards, nothing much had changed, and it had not seemed like a major issue. Once Gideon had moved his godfather in with him, they had done the crossword together over breakfast most days and enjoyed the odd game of chess in the evenings. Indeed, Gideon had been determined to manage the condition in his own way and keep his godfather at home with him for long as humanly possible.

Once Franklin had become too frail or forgetful to do most things for himself, a carer had been hired to come in once a day to help Franklin dress or to prepare a hot lunch for him, and for a few years things had gone smoothly enough, with only a few bad moments when Franklin had slipped out of the house unnoticed and got on a bus, heading heaven knows where...

It had been upsetting for Gideon, watching his favourite old gentleman deteriorate before his eyes. Things had begun to escalate in the last year: gas rings burning on high when he got home, saucepans of water left to boil dry, baths overflowing. Plus, several times Franklin had forgotten that he no longer ran the little bookshop in the High Street and had set off there on foot, once in his pyjamas and slippers, leaving the front door wide open.

But Number Seventeen, High Street, Merriweather, had long since been turned into a launderette, so Franklin had stood there among the noisy whirling machines, staring about in confusion, and demanding from surprised customers folding jeans or scooping out armfuls of warm, clean underwear what on earth had happened to his bookshop...

Eventually, Franklin himself had pleaded with Gideon to let him move into Five Oaks, the quiet residential care home situated a stone's throw from the busy street where he had lived and worked for most of his ninety-odd years.

Franklin already knew many of the other elderly residents, some of whom had even been at school with him, and there would be cared for twenty-four seven, with friendly and attentive staff, who would at least prevent him from wandering off and becoming unhappy and bewildered to find himself in a place he no longer recognised.

Gideon had agreed to let him go, albeit with guilt and misgivings.

'It's for the best,' everyone had told him, from the postwoman to his own boss at the veterinary surgery, and they were probably right.

He couldn't afford a full-time, live-in carer for Franklin. Yet the old gentleman couldn't be left alone for so long each day either. He would eventually have hurt himself. So Gideon had made his peace with the situation. If he could have given up work to look after Franklin full-time, he would happily have done so. But he would have been hurting others in the small community by abandoning his important work with animals, and he knew his grandfather would not have been much happier cooped up alone with his grandson all day.

The only saving grace was that Ophelia, his godfather's wife, had passed away five years ago, mere months before Franklin's diagnosis.

Ophelia had always been a trifle eccentric and had probably suffered from dementia herself, only in her case undiagnosed, with Franklin looking after her to the best of his ability. But at least she had been spared the horror of watching her beloved husband's slow decline too, instead succumbing to an attack of pneumonia brought on by foolishly dancing in the rain on her birthday night.

Gideon had dashed out and wrapped her in blankets as soon as he'd spotted the old lady twirling under the raindrops in a thin nightdress on a chilly October night, laughing merrily and clapping her hands. But the chesty cold that had followed that escapade had rapidly developed into pneumonia, and Ophelia had passed away in hospital less than two weeks later.

Franklin had suffered terribly after the loss of his wife, and it seemed likely that being widowed had hastened his own encroaching dementia. Not that Franklin had been obviously forgetful in the beginning, but he had made a few strange choices in his lifestyle that had led Gideon to suggest a trip to the doctor, such as storing his house keys in the fridge and staying up all night to write letters, of all things.

It was around that time that Gideon had moved permanently back to Cornwall, rather than simply visiting every few months. After Ophelia's passing, he had been determined to look after his lonely old godfather in his twilight years, for having lost his own parents early on, his childless godfather and Ophelia had taken him under their wing and Gideon had always felt strongly beholden to them both.

Of course, he could technically return to London now, if he wished. His godfather was being well cared-for at Five Oaks, after all, and since his memory did not always permit him to remember who Gideon was during his regular visits, not being on hand would hardly matter.

But that would have felt like a betrayal of Franklin's trust.

No, he would stay here in the small Cornish town of Merriweather, and continue to visit his godfather right up until the end, whether the old gentleman could recognise him or not.

He was working at the surgery tonight, he recalled, his footsteps slowing as he considered whether to return home for a bite to eat before heading to work or simply grab a sandwich on the hoof.

The veterinary surgery where he worked was at the far end of the High Street, so he would pass home on the way there. But he couldn't remember if there was anything left to eat in the fridge. Probably not. He wasn't very good at galvanizing himself to shop now that he lived alone…

There was a woman across the street, he realised, who was struggling to unlock the front door of the old florist shop. His steps slowed with sudden interest when he watched her muttering fury as the door shook in its frame but refused to open.

She was tall, maybe six foot, slim and angular with wide hips accentuated by the fitted summer dress she was wearing that nipped in at the waist and flared out at the knee. The yellow dress, covered in a haphazard pattern of lemons and pineapples, had narrow straps rather than sleeves, showing off a smooth tanned back and neat shoulders. Her hair fell to her shoulders and was platinum blonde, an unusual and striking colour that reminded him of someone, but he couldn't quite put his finger on it.

Without thinking about it, he waited for the next car to pass and then strolled across the road, hands in his pockets, and said in a friendly, off-hand way, 'Hello, you seem to be struggling with that door. Would you like a hand?'

The eyes that flashed a startled enquiry in his

direction were a wild, intense blue that seemed to look straight into him and beyond, into his psyche, his deep past, even his family tree. It was a disconcerting moment, like being stripped to the bone by a barracuda. Somehow he stayed upright.

But her smile was dazzling. 'Oh yes, I'd love a hand, thank you. This blasted door... I think maybe this is the wrong key. But the solicitor swore these were the only keys, and none of the others look like they would fit. So it has to be this one, doesn't it?' Still, she withdrew the key from the lock and studied it dubiously before handing it to him. 'Maybe you'll have better luck.'

'Maybe.' With a smile, Gideon slipped the key into the lock and lifted the door slightly so there was less strain on the mechanism. 'No luck involved though. You just need the knack.'

'The knack?'

Turning the key in the lock, he heard a click as it gave way, and the door swung open under a slight push.

'Like that.'

'Well, my goodness!' She stared at the open door. 'I certainly wish I had your...*knack*. Seems like a handy thing to possess.' The blonde grinned at him. 'I'm Penny, by the way. Thank you so much.'

She had thrust out a hand while speaking and Gideon found himself shaking it, taken aback by the strength of her grip.

'No need to thank me,' he insisted. 'I happen to know that the frame has shrunk and dropped over the years, so you need to lift at the same time as turning.'

'And how did you know that?' She looked him up and down, again with that searchlight stare. 'Are you a locksmith?'

'Good God, no.' He laughed. 'This shop belonged to an old friend of my godfather's. He was always in and out. That's how I know.'

Her eyes had widened. 'You knew my grandmother? Cecily?' When he nodded, she went on enthusiastically, 'She was my mum's mum, you see, and we didn't know much about that side of the family, because my mum passed away when I was little. But she must have known about me, because she left me this shop in her Will. I never knew her myself, though. Nobody told me she was still alive or I would have visited. I'm fascinated to meet anyone who actually knew her.'

'Yes, I knew her, though not very well. Only in terms of tagging along occasionally when my godfather came in here to buy flowers. They went back years, I think. Friends from school days. I'm so sorry for your loss.' He was still holding her hand, he realised belatedly, and let it go with a self-conscious smile. 'I'm Gideon. I'm a neighbour of yours.' He gestured vaguely at his house opposite, though it was set back from the road behind a hedge and she probably hadn't even noticed it. 'Welcome to Merriweather. And congratulations on your inheritance. Are you planning to stay or sell up?'

'Good question. And the straight answer is, I don't know.' She had big, honest eyes and that smile... It quite took his breath away. 'Sell up though, I should imagine. I'm pretty strapped for cash. And I know nothing about running a shop or living in Cornwall. Though I do know a bit about properties... Up until a year ago, I was working as an estate agent. Until they made me redundant.'

'That's bad luck. But at least you must know about market value and preparing a property for sale, and all that. Which is half the battle, I believe.'

'That,' she agreed with a twinkle in her eyes, 'and people having enough money to buy. It's a tough market right now, what with interest rates and the cost-of-living soaring. But I'm not greedy. I'll try to price it sensibly and hope for a quick sale.' She was peering inside the dim-lit shop now, clearly daunted by the thick shroud of dust over the tiled floor and surfaces, and the tsunami of junk mail piled up behind the door. 'Well, I'd best not keep you talking, Gideon. It was lovely to meet you but I'm sure you have better things to do. I think I need to find a broom and sweep this place clean first of all. And check through all this mail.'

'Actually, I'm on my way to work.' He saw her surprise and added quickly, 'I'm a vet... I work at the veterinary surgery just up the road here. Evening shift. Small animal surgery. Cats, dogs, even the odd rabbit or budgerigar. You'd be surprised what we get in the evening surgeries. Hurt paws, moulting feathers... Plus worms, of course.'

'Ugh.'

'So I will have to go, yes, but if you're in need of anything, I live right across the road at the Hollies.' Again, he indicated the house, and this time saw her gaze arrow in on the ramshackle, ivy-covered property. 'Don't worry, I always wash my hands after surgery. Soap and all.'

'Glad to hear it.' Impulsively, she shook his hand again, her face wreathed in smiles. Her platinum blonde hair swung like a shower of pale light about her shoulders. 'You're very kind, thank you. I may hold you to that. I've barely a clue what I'm doing right now, really. I've just spent a year backpacking around the globe. So my head is still in a totally different space.'

'I look forward to hearing about your adventures,' he said, waved his hand, and continued on down the road.

For some reason, he found himself whistling. He never whistled on his way to work. His steps were quick and light, and although he had felt quite despondent on leaving his godfather at the care home, wishing he could have the old gentleman back at home without Franklin suffering because of his long absences, he now felt as though a weight had been lifted from his shoulders.

How odd that a three-minute encounter could have changed his mood so drastically.

Penny.

The name suited her, informal and cheerful.

His mouth lifted at the corners into a quirky smile.

'Penny for your thoughts,' he murmured to himself as he turned up the drive into the vets. There, his smile rapidly fixed in place as a cacophony of barking and strained mewing reached his ears. He was five minutes late for evening surgery, and the waiting room was packed with customers and their owners. He recognised one tabby as an old, bad-tempered, inveterate biter, already glaring at him through the bars of her wicker basket.

'Once more unto the breach,' he called out to Sandra, who was seated with a disapproving expression behind the receptionist desk, but didn't stop to explain why, hurrying through to the examination room instead. 'Sorry I'm late. *Mea culpa.* Better send the first one through straightaway, thanks.'

'Good to see you *at last*, Gideon,' Sandra said with icy emphasis, and nodded to the lady with the tabby. 'The vet will see you now, Mrs Armitage. Apologies for keeping you waiting.'

Oops.

Fun time was over, he thought ruefully, heading for the sink in the prep area to scrub his hands and don his protective clothing. Time for work. And his stomach rumbled noisily, reminding him that he still hadn't found time for any dinner…

CHAPTER THREE

After removing the key and pretending to close the door after her useful visitor, Penny creaked it open it again and peeked out, gazing down the street after him in the late sunshine. Goodness gracious, Gideon had the nicest behind... And he was about her own height, which was pleasing. But he was dark and mysterious with it, and looked exceptionally hot in rolled-up shirtsleeves and smart-casual trousers.

A vet, too!

They were the cutest, weren't they? Good with animals, clearly kind and caring.

The perfect man, in fact.

And yes, she was totally ogling his rear view as he sauntered up the street.

Talking of rear views, at that very moment, Gideon half-turned to look back, as though sensing her glance.

Horrified, she ducked back inside the shop and shut the door so quickly the glass shook in its flame.

Her cheeks aglow with embarrassment, Penny

locked the door, grabbed up her rucksack and struggled through the narrow space at the back of the shop to the stairs that lay beyond. These led up to the first floor flat, the solicitor had explained to her on completing the paperwork, where Cecily had lived until the year or so prior to her death.

Mr Manton, pompous but friendly, had laboriously checked her ID, had her sign a few official documents, and then ceremoniously handed over the keys to the kingdom. He had seemed relieved to have the old property off his hands at last, though he'd had nothing but kind words to say about Cecily, and his smile had been sympathetic as Penny thanked him and made her way out.

Now the place was hers, to do with as she chose. It was surreal to go from having literally nothing in the world to owning a property, and she really didn't know what to do next.

She pushed the door open at the top of the stairs and heaved her rucksack inside, staring around in dismay. There was certainly plenty of cleaning to do. More dust up here too, she noted, though at least there were a few sticks of furniture in the flat, unlike in the shop below with its empty serving counter and display shelves.

A sofa heaped with stacks of yellowed newspapers and other items dominated the room while a round dining table – two chairs only – stood below the window. A dirty old sideboard ran along one wall, covered with dusty trinkets and debris. Drawn that way out of curiosity, Penny dropped her bag and stood examining the detritus of her unknown grandmother's life, hoping it would give her some clues as to that lady's personality and interests. But all she found were small china ornaments, bits of rubbish, and a few battered photo frames.

She picked up one photo frame and blew dust from it.

It was the photograph of a young woman in dungarees. At first glance, she thought it was a picture of *herself*, only with long blonde hair caught up in a ponytail, something she rarely bothered with. Then she realised it must be *her mum* at about the same age.

Fascinated, she devoured the photograph with her eyes for some time before reluctantly putting it aside and picking up another one.

This time, the photograph was more faded. It was also black-and-white and dated from the Fifties, she guessed, judging by the clothing.

Cecily herself, presumably.

She took the gilt-framed photograph to the curtained window and peered down at it in the soft early evening light.

A young woman sat on a garden wall, smiling into the camera with oddly familiar eyes and light-coloured hair. Not quite the spitting image of Penny's mum but clearly related. She knew that bold nose, for instance, and those big expressive eyes…

Beside her stood a young man with dark sleek hair, so sleek it was possibly Brycreemed to lie flat. They weren't hand-in-hand, but leaning against each other. Close friends then, if not lovers.

Penny studied the young man for a moment, wishing she knew who he was. But perhaps she would find more clues around the flat.

Penny put down the photo frame and finished her exploration. There wasn't much else to see though. It was a small flat, and besides a small shower room with WC, the only other space worth investigating was Cecily's bedroom. This was rather tidier than the living area. The mattress had been stripped and covered in plastic and seemed clean enough. There was a wardrobe packed with musty old clothes, some of which Penny brought out to admire or exclaim over in horror, and several drawers of the same, the contents jumbled up or spilling out onto the floor.

After her wanderings, she took out a sandwich she'd bought earlier, with a drink and a packet of crisps, and enjoyed a little picnic at one end of the sofa, pushing aside rubbish and old newspapers to perch on the edge there.

It wasn't the best of beginnings. But she hadn't expected much, anyway. In fact, she had expected the flat to be completely empty, with no personality. Just an empty shell she could smarten up and put on the market pretty much immediately. Instead, there was all... *this*.

It would involve a heck of a job, clearing all this stuff up, sorting out what she ought to keep and what ought to be thrown away. Though right now, she thought, glancing dismally at the heaps of newspapers that her grandmother appeared to have collected like a hoarder, she thought the bulk of it ought to be thrown away.

As she ate, her mind kept straying back to her grandmother and what it must have felt like, living alone in this tiny flat in her final years, knowing she had a granddaughter out there but not *where*.

It was heartbreaking, frankly, and she couldn't help a little sob.

Mr Manton, the solicitor, had told her they had taken such a long time to locate her because Cecily hadn't known her whereabouts, or even her date of birth, merely that a granddaughter existed. Which was odd in itself.

But since her mum had died while Penny was very young, she could only assume her dad hadn't bothered to inform the old lady when they'd moved house.

Dad had always claimed not to know of any living grandparents. But Penny didn't believe that anymore. Perhaps her dad had never got on with Cecily and had been glad to cut ties after Penny's mum died. That would seem the most likely situation. Not that it mattered now. It was far too late to make amends, she thought sorrowfully.

Now at least Penny had a chance to get to know Cecily, if only through this small flat and her most treasured belongings. Having seen the place and looked at those dusty framed photographs, she no longer intended to sell up immediately. Not without showing the old lady a proper amount of respect by getting to know who she'd been in life.

After all, Cecily could have bequeathed this flat to a charity, couldn't she? But instead, she had left all her worldly possessions to Penny, whom she had never met in her life.

Whatever the reasoning behind that odd but wonderful decision, it couldn't have been entirely financial. Could it?

Too weary and befuddled after a long first day in Merriweather to keep muddling out an unknown grandmother's thought processes, Penny dragged her trusty old sleeping bag from the rucksack, changed into pink bunny PJs, climbed into the bag's cosy warmth, and curled up to sleep…

It was morning when she finally awoke, disoriented to be in a strange place but aware that something specific had disturbed her dreams.

Someone was knocking on a door somewhere below her…

'What the hell…?'

Stumbling out of her sleeping bag, Penny caught her heel in the warm nylon folds, stumbled and almost knocked herself out on the wall.

'Ouch!'

Rubbing her sore head, Penny made her way precariously down the narrow stairs in her crumpled pyjamas. The dusty floor felt horrid on her bare feet, like she was picking up every piece of dust and dirt along the way – of which there were many thousands of specks! – until she stopped in the middle of the shop, staring at the door, embarrassed and uncertain.

Someone was indeed knocking at the door.

A man.

But she didn't recognise him. She had thought perhaps it was the solicitor, come to tell her something he'd forgotten yesterday, or possibly a delivery, though that was unlikely, given that she hadn't ordered anything, and nobody even knew she was here. Apart from the aforementioned solicitor.

Yet there was an old man framed in the shop doorway, his hand raised, knocking on the glass-panelled door.

He was tall but stooped, with thinning white hair and a strong, striking face. An aquiline nose, deep-set dark eyes peering into the shop with an urgent expression, mouth open as though saying something, repeating the same words again and again. He was dressed in a loose shirt topped with a baggy cardigan despite the heat, with slacks belted tightly at his narrow waist. He was so thin, she suspected those trousers might have fallen down without the belt.

As she stumbled towards the door, taking the key from the counter, the man stiffened almost in alarm, his eyes widening at the sight of her, and her gaze locked with his, curious to know what was wrong.

There was a brief pause in the traffic outside, which had been heavy and noisy, the road abruptly empty; suddenly, she was able to hear his voice.

'Cecily... Cecily.' That was what the old man was

saying, over and over, his eyes fixed on her face as though he couldn't believe what he was seeing. 'My God, Cecily, it's really you.'

A deep sense of foreboding swept over her.

Cecily?

She unlocked the door with a faltering hand and opened it a crack, peeping out at the old man. 'Um, hello,' she said, smiling in a reassuring manner, though she didn't feel terribly reassured herself. 'Can I help you?'

His hand shot out and gripped her wrist. He was surprisingly strong for a man his age. Which she guessed to be somewhere in his nineties. The deep-set eyes bored relentlessly into hers. 'Where have you been, Cecily? I've been looking for you for so long... For years and years.' He stared past her at the dusty shop with its empty shelves, the place sad and unlit. 'Have you been hiding in here all this time? And where are the flowers? Are you closing the shop?' His voice softened. 'I've been so worried about you. Didn't you get my letters?'

'I... I'm not Cecily.' Gently, she extricated herself from his grip. 'I'm her granddaughter.'

'What?' He stared at so wildly, she was almost afraid. Then he blinked and seemed to realise where he was and what he'd been saying. He took a step back and shook his head, repeating, 'Cecily's granddaughter? I didn't know... I'm sorry. So sorry.'

'It doesn't matter.' She opened the door wider, feeling awkward now. 'I would ask you inside. But there's nowhere to sit. I'm afraid the shop has been closed for some time now.'

He looked back at her, still blinking, clearly dazed. 'Yes, yes... It's been closed a long, long time. But where is Cecily?' His dark penetrating gaze lifted to her face again, and now she could see a terrible fear in those eyes. 'Tell me, please. I need to see her.'

Her heart thundering, Penny stammered, 'Well, she... I'm really sorry but the thing is... she's gone.'

'Gone? Where?'

'That is to say, I'm afraid that Cecily... Well, I'm afraid she passed over.' Penny swallowed, seeing the fear on his face, his lips parted, his eyes widening, fixed on her face. 'She died over a year ago. I'm terribly sorry. Was she a friend of yours?'

'Died? Oh my God. No, no...' Shaking her away when she tried to help him, the old gentleman stumbled away. A few doddering steps took him to the curb and then he was in the road, with a lumbering truck heading straight for him.

Appalled, Penny dashed after him. 'Careful!'

Before she could reach him though, a running figure had dashed past, scooping the old man up and drawing him back to safety on the pavement. The truck driver, who had stopped dead with a squeal of brakes, made a rude gesture at them both and then rumbled on along the road.

His rescuer was Gideon, the man she had met last night. That was when she remembered him saying that his godfather had known her grandmother.

This must be his godfather, she realised.

'Franklin, what on earth are you doing? The care

home phoned me at work... I know you get bored there. But you mustn't keep wandering off like this. You could have been killed just then.' Gideon sounded exasperated but not surprised. 'Didn't you see the truck coming?'

'No.' The old man ran a hand across his forehead, staring at Gideon as though not even sure who *he* was. 'I came to see Cecily. But she... *she* says that Cecily is dead.' He pointed round at Penny accusingly, who bit her lip in remorse. 'Why didn't you tell me, Gideon? Someone should have told me she was dead. I had no idea.' His voice rose. 'I should have gone to the funeral and paid my respects. It's not right that you hid this from me.'

'Look, let me walk you back to the care home, Franklin,' Gideon told him smoothly, 'and I'll explain everything on the way. Okay?'

Mouthing 'thank you' at Penny, he set off along the road, his arm about his godfather's waist, supporting the old gentleman as they made their way slowly back along the High Street.

Disturbed by this strange and unsettling encounter, Penny went back inside, locked the door, and climbed the stairs to change into day clothes. There was no electricity in the flat, so her first job today was to sort that out, get the utilities reconnected, and start sorting out the mess. But as she was dragging on her jeans and shirt, and belatedly brushing her hair in front of the dusty mirror, Penny was going over that strange meeting in her mind, wishing she had felt better prepared for that awkward conversation.

It was clear that Gideon's godfather and Cecily had been more than mere 'friends.'

But why had he mistaken her for Cecily?

Her grandmother had been in her mid-eighties when she died. It was true Penny didn't use as much moisturizer as she ought to, plus had skipped a few suncream sessions while in the hotter parts of the globe. But although she had freckles, her skin wasn't *that* aged by the sun.

And had Gideon really hidden Cecily's death from his godfather? That seemed rather cruel. But she didn't know the whole story, so she resolved to wait until she had more information before passing judgement.

Half an hour later, as she was sweeping up the dirty shop floor, Gideon knocked on the door and she opened it, smiling at him sympathetically. 'How's your godfather? I'm so sorry about what happened. I must have given the poor thing such a shock, telling him that Cecily had passed away.' She grimaced, trying not to sound judgy. 'I only wish I'd known that he wasn't in the loop, you know?'

'Oh, Franklin knew that Cecily had died. At the time, that is.' He pulled a face, seeing her confusion. 'My godfather suffers from dementia, I'm afraid. He went to Cecily's funeral. But he's forgotten.'

Light dawned at this explanation and she felt foolish. 'I see... Again, I'm so sorry. I wasn't aware of his condition.' Putting her broom aside, she beckoned him into the shop, closing the door behind him. It didn't seem like the sort of conversation you should have on the doorstep, she thought, shooting him an awkward smile. 'How is he? Not too shaken up by the bad news, I hope.'

'No, don't worry, he's fine. In fact, by the time I got him back to the care home, he'd already forgotten what you told him.' His eyes softened and he gave a faint half-smile. 'Dementia can be a blessing in that respect, I suppose. In his mind, Cecily is still alive and well.'

'Until I opened my big mouth!'

'You weren't to know,' he reassured her kindly.

She thought of that framed photograph upstairs in the flat. Cecily and the young, dark-eyed man. His godfather had looked uncannily like an older version of that youth.

'Were they close?' she asked, curious.

The smile disappeared and Gideon looked guarded again, sinking his hands into his trouser pockets. 'Close? I wouldn't say that, no.' But he looked away as he spoke, and she felt convinced he wasn't telling the truth. He shrugged, as though trying to make light of it. 'Anyway, thank you for talking to him. I hope he won't disturb you again. They really need to keep a better eye on the front door to the care home. It's usually kept locked but there was an unexpected delivery early this morning. Apparently, he slipped out while the receptionist was signing for parcels.' He shot her an apologetic smile, turning to the door. 'I'd better get back to work. See you again, no doubt.'

For the second time, she found herself instinctively ogling his trim behind as he left the shop, heading back towards the veterinary surgery. Gideon was striding, looking busy and in a hurry. But she had not missed that hint of annoyance in his eyes when she'd asked about his godfather's relationship with Cecily.

There was definitely some mystery there... But what?

Once the shop had been swept clean, all the debris removed from the floor and shelves, and the utilities reconnected, Penny felt she had made a good start to what she had mentally dubbed Operation Cecily. Proud of herself, despite an aching back, she strolled along to the local mini-supermarket to acquire more sandwiches, drinks, and crisps – despite this being her second day of unhealthy eating – and retreated to the flat, where she had cleared off the sofa and dusted the table ready for use.

After this meagre but affordable meal, she heaved a deep sigh of resignation and launched herself at the sideboard with its cupboards and drawers bulging with jumbled up items. It was mostly dreary work, discarding old tat and bits of rubbish. But eventually her determination to get to know her grandmother better was rewarded with a treasure trove... For there, in a small tin pushed to the back of the righthand cupboard, she found a stack of letters, opened but still in their envelopes, all addressed to her grandmother in the same bold, masculine hand and signed merely with an initial.

My dearest Cecily, the first one began, *I know you don't approve of my writing to you like this. But I miss you madly. You are the light in my sky, the lift in my step, the wave bearing my lost soul home...*

Her eyes widened.

Love letters, without a doubt! And presumably an illicit love too. Otherwise, why on earth would Cecily not have approved of him writing to her?

It felt odd glancing through her grandmother's old love letters. Like eavesdropping on a deeply intimate conversation without permission. But Cecily was long gone, and presumably she had left these letters for someone – if not her granddaughter, then who? – to discover and read after she'd passed away.

As she read, a nagging suspicion planted itself in her head that Cecily had left this tin of private letters here deliberately, hoping that someone would find out about their romance after she'd gone. Like leaving behind a testimony.

'F,' she muttered, tracing the large black initial that closed all the letters. Though she noticed how some of the letters, mostly towards the bottom of the pile, were decidedly shakier, the handwriting more sloping and messier, the initial less bold than in the beginning. As though the writer were getting older...

What were the odds that 'F' was Gideon's godfather, Franklin?

CHAPTER FOUR

As Gideon walked past the old florist shop on his way home from work, he felt embarrassed. It wasn't his fault that his godfather had accosted Cecily's granddaughter and had to be escorted back to the care home. Yet he couldn't help feeling guilty. The poor young woman had only just arrived in Merriweather, no doubt still grieving for her grandmother, and it must have been a shock to have a stranger yelling at her like that. Worse, he had seen, from across the street, how his grandfather had caught her arm. Some people might consider that assault these days. Thank goodness, she had not been offended. And somehow, he had managed to dash across in front of that oncoming truck and save Franklin from being knocked down. That would have been an absolute disaster. The old gentleman was frail enough as it was and would never have survived a road accident. But tragedy had thankfully been averted and the nurses at the home had apologized and sworn they would keep a better watch on Franklin from now on...

Exhausted after a long day, he decided cooking was beyond him and he would grab a Chinese meal instead, and was just stepping out of his front door on his way to the local takeaway when he realised that he had a visitor.

Cecily's granddaughter was walking up the garden path towards his door.

Even dressed casually in tight-fitting jeans and a white vest top, Penny was eye-catching enough to make him stop and take a deep breath.

'Hello again,' he said in surprised tones, hurrying to pin a smile to his lips. It was stupid to feel guilty after that debacle with Franklin earlier. But he couldn't help it. 'Are you having a problem?' He assumed she had come over to ask for help with something, given he was probably the only person she knew in Merriweather. 'Happy to help.'

He could have kicked himself for adding that. It sounded like something idiotic on a work tape barred or name badge. *Happy to help.*

Good grief.

To his relief though, she didn't seem to have noticed that he was babbling nonsense. In fact, she was holding out a rusty, battered tin. The sort of tin that came with biscuits at Christmas. These ones had been shortbread. Gideon doubted she was offering him aeons-old-old festive shortbread though. Not given her tense expression.

'You need to read these,' she told him, her tone urgent, hand outstretched.

'I'm sorry?'

'I found this old tin in the flat. It's full of letters. Love letters from someone called signing himself F, written to my grandmother,' she went on, her gaze fixed dramatically on his face. Her eyes really were the deepest blue, he thought, feeling dazzled and off balance. 'F wouldn't happen to be your godfather, would it?' She raised sharp thin brows. 'F for Franklin?'

This question knocked him sideways. Blinking, Gideon dragged himself back to reality. What was she saying?

F... for Franklin.

He looked at the closed tin and then back at her face, saying slowly, 'Actually, yes. I believe Franklin did write to Cecily quite regularly at one stage. He was in the army when he was younger and often away from home. They were friends before he married.' A warning bell went off at the back of his head as he worked through what she was saying, and he shifted automatically into defensive mode. 'Sorry, did you say *love* letters?'

'That's right.'

He squared his shoulders. 'Ah, then you must be mistaken. Franklin and Cecily were always just friends.'

Her lips tightened and again she thrust the tin towards him. 'If that's what you think, you really ought to read them yourself, in that case.'

'Why would I need to read them? They're private letters. None of our business. Besides, my godfather hasn't been able to write his own name in years, let alone pen a whole letter. So whatever's in that tin must be ancient history.' He stuck his chin out. 'Not worth bothering about, in my opinion.'

'Let the past stay in the past? Is that what you're saying?' There was a challenge in her face. Goodness, she was tall for a woman. Almost on his eye level. It was disconcerting.

'Something like that,' he agreed, aware that he was being difficult but unable to help it. Uneasiness flooded him and he shifted under her accusing gaze. Whatever was in that tin, they should dispose of it, he decided. And the sooner the better. 'Raking up the past… What's the point? You'll only cause trouble.'

'Trouble? With whom?'

He couldn't answer that, but set his lips, meeting her gaze steadily without saying a word. She was a newcomer; she couldn't understand how much people in a place like this loved to gossip. And it was down to him to protect his godfather's reputation.

His glare didn't stop her going on blithely, 'Anyway, not all these letters are old. They're not all dated but one or two are. Including some written as recently as five years ago.'

He frowned. 'Impossible.'

'Why do you say that?'

She was persistent, he had to give her that.

Gideon took another deep breath to steady himself. 'Well, apart from the indisputable fact that Franklin was diagnosed with dementia five years ago, he was also happily married at the time.' He paused, aware that he wasn't being entirely truthful. 'That is, his wife Ophelia did actually die five years ago,' he added reluctantly. 'But he was grieving. A broken man. Indeed, I'm sure her loss precipitated his dementia. So he wouldn't have been writing love letters to anyone after Ophelia died.' He paused, noting that she still didn't seem satisfied. 'In other words,' he added firmly, 'you must be mistaken. Either those letters are from some other "F" or they're not... not *love letters*.'

'So prove it. Read them.'

He glanced at the tin, his teeth grinding together. 'I'd rather not,' he admitted. 'Stuff like that ... they're not my thing.'

'Love letters aren't your thing?'

He hissed out an exasperated breath. 'I didn't mean it like that.'

'Good. Then will you at least take a look at these letters?' she asked, still holding out the tin. Her voice was both pleading and indignant, as though she couldn't quite believe that he had refused her original request. 'Just a few of them?"

Feeling cornered, Gideon sank his hands into his pockets and rocked back on his heels. 'I suppose I could do that,' he agreed reluctantly. He wasn't happy about the situation. He had a suspicion that reading those letters might stir up a hornets' nest in his quiet, perfectly ordered life. But it was equally clear to him that this woman would not give up easily. Humouring her might be the best way forward. 'Better leave the tin with me, then. I'll have a rummage through it when I get time and pick out one or two to read. No promises, mind.'

'Oh no, that's not going to happen. I'm not letting these letters out of my sight.' His new neighbour tucked the tin under her arm and raised her chin. She was flushed and defiant, and extraordinarily attractive. There was a vivacity about her that reminded him of her grandmother, who had also possessed those spirited blue eyes and stubborn chin, fighting for what was right even in her last years.

'I see.' He gave a sigh and shook his head, giving up. 'I presume that means you want us to look at the letters together.'

'Pretty much, yes.' She paused, considering. 'Though I could *photograph* them and send you the files.'

Gideon's eyebrows rose. 'I don't think we need to be that cold-blooded about it, surely? They're not state secrets.'

She visibly relaxed, smiling faintly. 'I suppose not. But these letters are precious to me. They're all I have left of my grandmother. I didn't know her, remember? So I don't want them getting lost or damaged.'

'I can understand that.' He hesitated, aware of a nagging sympathy for her predicament. 'How about we look at them over dinner?'

'Okay. When?'

'Right now works for me. I was just popping out for a Chinese takeaway, in fact. I could get enough for two and you could join me.' He jerked his thumb over his shoulder, indicating the house. 'What do you say?'

At this impromptu suggestion, she looked taken aback and even a little suspicious. 'Have dinner with you? Erm, I don't know.' Her brows tugged together. 'Won't your wife – or girlfriend – mind if I join you for dinner?'

'I have neither a wife nor a girlfriend. So we're good.'

'Oh.'

This candid information seemed to disconcert her even more. But perhaps she thought his offer of dinner was a proposition. And maybe it was.

Suppressing a grin, he glanced at his watch. 'Look, I'm starving and it's past my dinner time. Beef chow mein? Sweet-and-sour chicken? Or are you a veggie?'

'No, I eat meat…' She bit her lip and gave a quick shrug, looking away. 'The thing is, I don't have much cash on me. In fact, I don't have any cash at all.' Her cheeks reddened even further. 'To tell you the truth, I'm flat broke. All I have is that old shop that Cecily left me. I did have some redundancy money left but I spent the last of it travelling down to Cornwall. The rest went on a backpacking holiday.' She looked embarrassed. 'Not the most sensible thing to do with my redundancy money, I know. But it was my life's dream, you see. Only it turns out that dreams can be rather expensive.'

Gideon knew he shouldn't be amused by her pecuniary troubles. But he couldn't help a tiny chuckle at the thought of her spending redundancy money on a globe-trotting holiday. Seeing her chin go up, he said quickly, aware that laughter at her predicament had probably been rude and inappropriate, 'Don't worry about it. It's my treat. Look, why don't you go inside and make yourself at home? You'll find most things in obvious places in the kitchen. Make a cup of tea or grab a chilled bottle of beer from the fridge. Lay the table for two. I'll be about fifteen or twenty minutes, depending on the queue. Is that acceptable?'

Her smile was a wonder to behold, truly lighting up her face. 'That's very generous of you, Gideon. Thank you, in that case I… I'd be delighted.' She bit her full lower lip again, the movement catching his eye. 'I've eaten nothing but sandwiches and crisps for the past forty-eight hours. A Chinese takeaway sounds like heaven.'

'Back soon,' he promised, and pressed the house keys into her hand with a grin. 'How about a big bag of prawn crackers on top, yes?'

Stunned by Gideon's generosity, not to mention his trusting nature in allowing her – essentially a complete stranger he'd only just met – free rein in his home, Penny waited until he'd vanished down the high street, and then let herself in through the front door.

She stood a moment in the spacious hall, drinking in the gorgeous scents of floor polish and fresh flowers and the masculine hint of citrus aftershave.

The hall was dark wood-panelled, a grandfather clock standing proudly at one end, its heavy gold pendulum tick-tocking majestically back and forth. Cream carpeted stairs lead up into the soft glow of evening light on an upper landing, framed oil paintings lining the walls at discreet intervals. She got the distinct impression of wealth and comfort, but more than that, a sense of home and happiness. Or potential happiness, at least.

Abruptly, an image flooded her mind, of small kids running through the hall, laughing and playing, with Gideon chasing after them, grinning exactly as he'd done on passing her the keys just now...

No wife or girlfriend.

At his age, and given his looks, a lack of attachment could mean he had personality or other issues stopping him from attracting women. Or it could merely be a sign that he was a loner and a serial one-night-stander. She wasn't sure where she stood on either of those situations.

But this was only dinner.

Wasn't it?

Closing the front door behind her with a soft click, Penny tiptoed down the hall, peeking into rooms with intriguingly open doors, finding a lovely sitting room with plush sofas and more clocks on the mantle and beautiful arrangements of dried flowers in large vases; a pantry with shelves from floor to ceiling; a downstairs loo and shower; a small book room with a desk and chair overlooking a pretty back courtyard with a stone statue and fountain playing against a backdrop of white roses; and finally, down a short flight of steps, the kitchen itself.

A range took up one wall, a huge wondrous beast with two large red lids, though it didn't seem to be on, thankfully, given the recent heat they'd been enduring. There was also a state-of-the-art modern cooker and stove – she wondered if he ever used the range for cooking – a dishwasher, washing machine and tumble dryer, and glass-fronted kitchen cupboards stacked neatly with cups, glasses, plates and bowls et cetera.

She had not noticed a dining room on her way through the house, but the kitchen was large enough to hold a circular table covered with a white tablecloth. Impressed both by Gideon's immaculate housework and attention to detail, she hunted through drawers and soon found cutlery, table mats, and glasses, laying the table as requested for two people eating. She also found spoons for serving from takeaway boxes and a drawer full of neatly laundered and folded cloth napkins.

Finally, she filled the kettle and put it on to boil, found tea bags and a teapot, and made tea for two, bringing it to the table with two mugs. Though she didn't know if he would prefer beer instead. Opening the fridge, she found it not particularly well stocked with food, but with a section dedicated to beer cans and bottles. She didn't drink beer herself but withdrew a bottle, found a bottle opener and tall glass, and placed them on the table next to the setting where she imagined he might wish to sit.

It was only at that point that she realised the intimacy of the situation. The curious domesticity of what she was doing. Short of finding candles and lighting them, or putting on soft music in the background, this could almost be a date.

And why not?

Her chin went up defiantly.

She was a free agent and Gideon was most definitely her type. The right height, the right colouring, and the kind of quirky, charismatic personality that she enjoyed clashing with. And he lived in a wonderful house and was undoubtedly solvent, which was not something found very often in the temporary boyfriends she'd made on the road. Most of them had been out of work or travelling the world like herself. Certainly not high-earning, stable pillars of the community like Gideon.

Firmly, she told herself she shouldn't count her chickens before they were hatched. Yes, Gideon had said 'no wife' and 'no girlfriend' but he might... Well, he might be gay and involved with a man! How could she possibly know?

Still, it was tempting to let her imagination drift about their own potential friendship, and she found herself humming as she tidied the knife and fork beside each place setting, arranging the tin of love letters in the middle of the table like a centrepiece. Ready for after they'd eaten.

'That looks amazing,' Gideon said, close behind her, and she jumped, turning with a startled expression, not having heard him come in.

'Thank you. I... I wasn't sure if you wanted beer or tea,' she stammered, and willed her stupid cheeks to stop blushing. She only hoped he had not been able to read her mind. Or her happy humming... 'In the end, I gave you both.'

'Good idea,' he said, placing the bag of Chinese on the kitchen counter and beginning to unpack it. 'Tea with the meal, beer after?' He unpeeled the lid of a steaming pot of chow mein, its rich tasty smell filling the room. 'Mmm, this looks good.'

They sat down to eat together and barely spoke, focused on the meal. The Chinese food was delicious and very filling. Indeed, she could not remember even having eaten such a tasty meal. But hunger always was the best sauce, wasn't it?

Afterwards, she could hardly move, and did not object when he suggested coffee in the living room. 'What a good idea.'

The room he led her to was cosy and intimate. More of a snug than a living room, Penny thought, collapsing thankfully onto soft red sofa cushions. He disappeared for a while, coming back with a tray. Smiling, he handed her a dainty cup on a saucer, the fragrant coffee generously laced with cream, and sat next to her on the sofa. Her senses prickled at his proximity, but she managed a smile, pushing such inappropriate feelings aside. She barely knew him, after all. And given that they were now neighbours, starting something too hastily could mean rather too much repenting in leisure, as the saying went.

'I suppose we'd better make a start looking at these letters,' Penny said, mostly to distract her overactive brain. Putting her coffee down after one hasty sip, she reached for the tin of letters she'd placed on the coffee table before them. 'Shall I read one out loud?'

CHAPTER FIVE

She had expected a protest. Gideon said nothing but shrugged, crossing one leg over the other, his body language convincing her of his reluctance. All the same, since he didn't actively refuse, she prised the lid off the old biscuit tin and selected one of the letters at random. She had read a number of letters before coming across the road to see him, of course, but only dipping in and out, none of them all the way through. So she was curious to get a proper feel for them.

Feeling nervous, perhaps because of his silence, perhaps because she was delving into someone else's intimate past, she cleared her throat before beginning to read aloud from the letter in her hand. *'Dearest Cecily, I know you said we shouldn't keep writing to one another. But I can't help doing so. The thought of never being able to open up to you again, to explore the hope and the anguish in my heart, feels like the worst kind of torture. I say torture because it goes so deep in me. Deep as the soul...'*

'All right, let me stop you right there,' Gideon said abruptly, shifting at last.

He had been drinking his black coffee while she read the letter aloud, but now placed the dainty cup and saucer on the table beside hers. A frown knitted his dark brows together and he looked rather forbidding. She could almost imagine him with a cane in his hand, like an old-fashioned schoolteacher. The thought made her jump inwardly, and then blush at the naughtiness of that thought. Goodness, her brain was a cesspit!

'What's the date on that letter?' he went on in the same tough voice.

'The date?' Penny blinked and dragged herself back to reality, surprised by his response. 'Why? Is it important?'

'Of course it's important. Don't you get it?' When she stared at him, bemused, he added grimly, 'Up until five years ago, my godfather was married. Now do you understand?'

'Oh,' she said.

'Oh, indeed.' Gideon ran a hand through sleek dark hair and looked away, his jaw tense. 'Impossible to ask him now, I guess. Cruel too, given his dementia. But I refuse to believe he could ever have been unfaithful to his wife.' He considered it for a moment, and then shook his head. 'No, not Franklin. He wasn't that kind of husband.'

She understood immediately and sympathised. It must be horrid for him, imagining that his godfather could ever have betrayed his marriage vows. Yet, at the same time, it was potentially horrid for her too. She was only just getting to know her late grandmother. Had Cecily been the sort of woman who would knowingly carry on with another woman's husband behind her back? With a shudder, she pushed that unpleasant thought away. She couldn't believe it either.

Hurriedly, she studied the letter and heaved a sigh of relief. 'It's dated three years ago,' she told him. 'You said that your godfather's wife –'

'Her name was Ophelia.'

'I'm sorry, of course. You said Ophelia passed away five years ago? But this letter is dated *after* that. So, you don't need to worry that Franklin was being unfaithful behind his wife's back by writing to Cecily.' She showed him the dated letter as proof. 'He was already a widower by the time he wrote this.'

Gideon did look relieved, though not entirely happy about the situation. 'I suppose that does change things. And I'm glad… Though I'm not sure I understand why he was writing to her at all. Franklin always told me… Well, this is before he began to lose his memory, it's true. But he would say how much he adored Ophelia. Given that, it seems strange he would have been carrying on with your grandmother.'

'Writing letters is hardly *carrying on*,' she pointed out mildly.

'But the way that letter starts… It was hardly a platonic relationship, was it?' He drank more coffee, clearly troubled. 'And at their age too. It seems odd, that's all I'm saying.'

Penny could see that he was struggling with the idea of his godfather starting a new relationship with anyone in his twilight years. Which was dreadfully ageist to her mind. But perhaps there was more to it than mere prejudice.

'I think we should read these letters properly,' she suggested. 'From start to finish. Maybe the answers you seek are here, but we'll need to look at them all.' His brows had risen again. As brows went, his were surprisingly mobile. Up, down, up, down. She tried not to stare at them. 'Okay, perhaps not *all of them* if you don't have time tonight... But I think we should study a few at least, rather than jump to conclusions.'

She had expected him to refuse. But, still looking frustrated, Gideon shrugged and admitted, 'You're probably right. We won't know more without reading his letters to her. It makes me uncomfortable, that's all. I've always thought of Franklin as a one-woman man. Now I hear this and I don't know what to think. It's unexpected, I guess.'

'I'm so sorry. I can perfectly see why you might be upset –'

'Upset?' Gideon frowned and stiffened, appearing offended by her choice of word. No doubt he didn't see himself as a man who ever got 'upset'. 'I'm not upset. I'm disappointed, perhaps. And a little disbelieving. I'm not sure we've understood their relationship properly. Maybe they were just friends after all, and Franklin was just into... flowery language.'

'Come on.' She raised her own eyebrows at him, quietly reading aloud the emotional first few lines of the letter again. 'Does that sound like they were *just friends*?' she asked on finishing.

He hesitated, peering into his coffee cup as though the answers lay there. 'It sounds as though Cecily was less interested in Franklin than he was in her,' he said slowly, and his gaze shifted to meet hers.

His eyes really were the most intense and velvety dark she had ever seen.

A frisson ran through her and she had to look away. Her heart was beating so rapidly, it felt like a bird trapped in her chest. Which was a flowery enough image for even one of Franklin's love letters…

Thankfully, Gideon could not read minds. His voice was neutral as he went on, 'Perhaps you're right and we should read a few more letters. To get the full picture.' He paused. 'Though I'd really like to see any letters Cecily wrote back to him. Replies she made to these letters.'

'Agreed,' she said, nodding enthusiastically.

He stretched out one arm along the back of the sofa, half invading her space. Not that she minded that. But she did wonder if he was doing it deliberately. A kind of silent flirtation. There was a half-smile on his lips as he nodded. 'Well?'

Taking this as permission to keep going, Penny picked up the letter again and found her place. She was a little annoyed to realise her hand was trembling. This was hardly the first time she'd indulged in a flirtation with a near-stranger. But something about this man made it different. Gideon was simply so solid and so deeply charismatic, she couldn't imagine him bothering to mess her about. Not like all the rest.

'*It still feels like yesterday when we first met,*' she continued to read aloud. '*Though it must be seventy-odd years ago now. A lifetime for some people. And I still regret my choices. If I had the chance to do it all again, would I do things differently? Yes, absolutely. But I was young and stupid, and in those days I didn't know a good thing when I saw one. You were that good thing, Cecily.*'

She paused, seeing Gideon's face change as he listened to that romantic line, but went on, a slight tremor in her voice at the enormity of what she was reading, '*I loved Ophelia with all my heart. That is undeniable. But, at the back of my head, I always knew you and I ought to have been together. It makes me feel guilty, writing that down. It feels like a betrayal of my late wife. Yet if I hadn't gone off with Ophelia that night, simply because I saw you and Peter at the fair together and became stupidly jealous, perhaps we would have got past that bad moment. Then we would have spent our lives together instead. But Ophelia fell pregnant from that one careless mistake – all my fault, I readily accept the blame – and I did the right thing by her, even though she lost the baby after we married and it was all for nothing. Ophelia was a wonderful woman and the best wife any man could ever hope for. And I was careful never to let my thoughts stray back to you while I was married.'* She paused, clearing her throat as a lump of emotion clogged it. *'But I can't deny the yearnings of my heart, not now that Ophelia has gone. Can you forgive the mistakes of the past, my dearest Cecily? Can you forgive me for being a jealous fool? Is it too late for us to be together in these final years? Please let me know. Your loving friend forever, Franklin.'*

'Good God,' Gideon muttered.

'Pretty amazing stuff, isn't it?' Penny agreed, folding up the old letter and placing it to one side, so they would know it had been read. 'I wonder if she could, though? Forgive the mistakes of the past, that is.'

Gideon leant forward and buried his face in his hands for a few minutes. 'I genuinely have no idea. But I can't believe what I'm hearing.' He sat back, gazing at her questioningly. 'So Franklin and Cecily were involved before he even married Ophelia? I don't know what to think about that.'

Penny chewed on her lip, equally bemused. 'I didn't know Cecily. But if I had done, I would probably feel the same as you do about all this. There's obviously a lot more to their relationship than met the eye.' She picked up another letter, unfolding it speculatively. This one was longer, two sheets, both sides covered with dense black handwriting. 'Do you feel strong enough to hear another one?'

'Frankly, no. But what choice do I have?' Gideon gave a groan and then leaped to his feet. 'I tell you what, before you launch into another letter, let's make a night of it.'

Her eyes widened, her mouth suddenly dry. 'I... I beg your pardon?'

He laughed, seeing her shocked expression. 'Dirty mind! I didn't mean it like that. I was just suggesting we should crack open a bottle of wine.'

'Oh.'

Without waiting for her to gather her scattered thoughts, he collected the coffee cups and jug of cream with an efficient hand and strode to the door. 'I may have a chocolate cake in one of the cupboards too, if you like that kind of thing.' He cocked a dark eyebrow at her. 'Or we could share a bowl of peanuts. Sweet and salty...' His voice was suggestive.

She bit back a gurgle of laughter. 'Erm, sweet and salty sounds good.'

'I don't have to work tomorrow morning and I'm presuming you're not working either while you're here. So, unless you mind staying up late while we work through these letters together, you could... I don't know.... stay over?' His gaze met hers and lingered. 'I have a guest room and I'm willing to bet it's more comfortable than the flat above the old flower shop.'

Penny's heart turned somersaults at the teasing smile in his eyes. She had thought him a little harsh earlier, talking about Franklin and her grandmother as though accusing them of not behaving properly. But she could see that his initial surprise had given way to resignation, and he was now as fascinated as she was by this secret history. She liked that about him, how he was open to having his mind changed…

Plus, much as she was prepared to love Cecily for leaving her the flower shop, he was dead right about the flat.

'You had me at wine,' she admitted, smiling shyly.

CHAPTER SIX

His godfather's letters to Cecily, the sweet, rather doddery eighty-something florist whom he had known since childhood, were a complete revelation to Gideon. For all the years he'd known Cecily, he had seen her merely as a cheerful old lady and a good friend of his godfather's, always ready with a smile and an excellent recommendation for flowers to suit any social or personal occasion.

Secretly, he had thought dear old Cecily ought to have retired years ago – even decades ago! – but also rather admired her doughty work ethic. Besides, he had supposed the demands of her shop must be small enough not to be beyond her scope. After all, she had only been open two days a week in the five or so years before she finally retired. And the younger professionals in Merriweather tended to use the big florist chain in the next town or order online these days, so Cecily had catered mostly to the older generation or had taken chance orders from passing customers who needed flowers locally and in a hurry, or who'd spotted one of her lovely floral arrangements in the window and had stopped to buy them.

And if his godfather had frequently lingered in her dusty old shop for a natter or gone up into her flat to take tea or dinner with her now and then, what of it?

The two had been friends 'forever' as Franklin had always pointed out and what could be more natural than two elderly people of roughly the same age spending time together, gently reminiscing about the 'old days'?

Now, those hours spent above the shop felt somehow sinister or not quite respectable, which was ridiculous, he freely admitted it. Franklin was a widower and Cecily herself had long been a widow, and surely both had been beyond the age of strong physical passions. And yet… he couldn't feel comfortable about it. It was almost as though they'd been carrying on illicitly behind his back. Behind everyone's backs, in fact. For they'd never been open about their true relationship, had they? It now looked as though they'd been *friends with benefits*, not mere old friends.

Unless he was reading the situation wrongly.

'Still,' as he remarked to Penny after she dabbed at her eyes and folded the final letter away into that damn biscuit tin, 'we can't be sure what Cecily thought of all this correspondence. We don't have her replies. Only his letters to her.'

'But he often mentions her letters to him,' she pointed out with an audible sniff – she'd been freely sobbing at times while reading, so much so that he'd been forced to take over reading the letters aloud during her most emotionally incontinent moments – 'and passes comment on her views and attitudes. So we know she definitely wrote back. Maybe even replied in person when they met up.' She rattled the tin at him. 'And she kept these, didn't she? If they were unwelcome, wouldn't she simply have thrown them out?'

'Good point.' He glanced at his watch, hearing the old grandfather clock in the hall chiming the hour. 'Midnight.' He drained his wine glass and looked furtively at her own. 'Want to open another bottle?'

'Goodness, no! I need to go to bed.'

Remembering belatedly that he was the host, Gideon got up at once. 'Of course. You must be exhausted. I'll go and make up the bed in the guest room, unless you'd like a nightcap or hot drink before bed?'

'Thank you, no.' She was looking uncertainly at the door, as though planning to weave across the road back towards the flat above the old flower shop.

He didn't like that idea.

Quickly, hoping to encourage her to stay, he said persuasively, 'There's a new pack of toothbrushes in the bathroom that I keep for moments like this. Feel free to break into it. Toothpaste on the side. Towels in the bathroom cupboard.'

She thanked him, following him awkwardly upstairs. He couldn't be sure why he was so intent on keeping her in his house overnight – he certainly had no intention of making a pass at her!– but he liked the idea of seeing her comfortable tonight at least. He was convinced that Cecily's flat – which he remembered as small and damp even when she was living there – could hardly be a nice place to stay. It was a neighbourly thing to do, that was all, offering her nicer accommodation…

Oh yes, a sarcastic voice told him as he fetched fresh linen from the airing cupboard, you've asked her to stay overnight so she won't be uncomfortable. Not because you want to keep her under your roof for as long as possible.

He glowered inwardly at that nasty voice, and swiftly made up the bed for her while Penny was in the bathroom, discreetly washing, brushing and gargling, a shadowy form behind the frosted glass panels. He wasn't interested in her that way, he told himself sternly, and almost laughed out loud at how ludicrous he was being. Of course he was!

But he wasn't an ogre, and she was his guest.

Some previous visitor – an old uni friend of his – had left behind a pair of pale blue silk pyjamas, which he'd conscientiously had laundered. These he now laid across the guest bed, certain they would fit even tall Penny, for his friend was only a little shorter.

'Oh, those are pretty,' she exclaimed, appearing in the doorway. There was a tiny hint of suspicion behind her words that made him explain, inexplicably embarrassed, about his forgetful friend. 'Thank you. That's very thoughtful of you.'

'No problem.' He edged towards the door, suddenly aware of her feminine scent mixed with a hint of spearmint toothpaste, a smell he really liked, always so clean and fresh…

'Goodnight,' she said, her gaze on his.

'Yes, goodnight. Sleep well.' And without really knowing what he was doing, Gideon found himself bending his head to kiss her goodnight. On the lips!

Not that he had to bend far, they were so close in height. And though she gave a small gasp of shock as their lips met, hers soon parted, her arms rising to link about his neck as the kiss deepened.

Almost as soon as it had begun, the kiss was over. He drew back, flushed and more than a little shocked by his own behaviour, sucking in a breath. 'God, I'm so sorry…. I didn't mean… It wasn't my intention…' He was babbling, Gideon realised, and cut himself off with an abrupt, 'See you in the morning, then.'

Penny said nothing but stared after him in obvious amazement as he hurried away. Her own colour had been heightened, he realised, and hardly surprising, the way he'd grabbed her without warning.

Gideon swore under his breath as he dived into his bedroom and shut the door, aware that he'd badly wanted to stay and kiss her some more. But they'd only just met and his own past experiences of instant attraction – and its inevitable consequences – warned him to be cautious, that he could end up locked into an embarrassing situation with a neighbour, simply because he'd been unable to control his instincts.

He stood a moment, frowning, eyes shut.

Franklin's letters...

We can't be sure what Cecily thought of all this correspondence. We don't have her replies.

An old memory tugged at him, and he caught his breath in shock. Was it possible her replies to Franklin were *under this very roof*?

Making her way downstairs the next morning, guided by the delicious smell of bacon frying, Penny slipped into the kitchen to find her host already cooking breakfast. This morning, he was dressed in jeans and a tight-fitted tee-shirt that moulded to strong upper arms and tight abs, absolutely drawing the eye. Well, her eye, at least. Both eyes, in fact. Yes, she was ogling the poor man again, and abruptly looked away as he turned, seeing her come in. Good grief. What must he think of her, constantly staring at him?

Though after last night...

She hadn't dreamt it, she reminded herself. He had kissed her good night. And not in a platonic, neighbourly way. More in a 'come to bed' way.

But he had clearly changed his mind within seconds, for he'd broken off the kiss almost immediately and scurried away to bed.

Perhaps her breath had been all wine and Chinese food. Maybe she'd had noodle strands in her teeth. Oh God...

Embarrassment flooded her yet again at such a terrible possibility, and she stammered, 'Good morning.' And promptly walked into the table leg, trying to avoid standing too close to him. 'Ouch!'

Concern flashed across his face as he studied her, frying spatula raised. 'You okay?'

'Yes, fine. I love stubbing my toe in the mornings. It's such an effective way to wake up.' Her smile turned wan as he stared, no doubt thinking her crazy. 'Sleep well? Yes, I slept well. Very well, in fact. That bed is very, um, comfortable.'

In fact, she had spent hours tossing and turning, remembering his kiss, and wondering what had put him off, and if she ought to have gone after him, or if her correct choice of response ought to have been to slap his face. What was the etiquette in these situations? When you barely know someone and they make a pass which isn't entirely unwelcome? She had no idea, having usually either gone with her gut and not worried about the consequences or backed away with a polite, 'No, thank you.'

This time she had been the one left hanging, uncertain of his feelings and motivation, and wishing she had the courage to tiptoe down the hall and tap at his door...

But that would have been outrageous behaviour.

And potentially dangerous.

She didn't know Gideon properly, had only just met him, and she wasn't backpacking now, where chance-met strangers might never be seen again if things didn't work out. This man was well-known in this community and lived right opposite the property she'd just inherited. Even if she put it straight on the market, she would likely hang around here while it was for sale rather than go home where she wasn't wanted. Basically, the chances of seeing this man again after a one-night-stand were so high, they were practically on the roof.

So, the mature way to play this budding relationship would be *cautiously*. Assuming she could remember how to be cautious… Besides which, he was older than her. Not vastly older, but old enough to make her worry they would have little in common and nothing to talk about once this letters situation was over.

'Breakfast?' he asked her casually, unfastening his chef's apron.

'Thank you, yes,' she readily agreed, though the last thing she felt like doing after such a difficult night was munching her way through a plate of bacon and eggs. But the smell was delicious and, besides, it would have been horribly rude to refuse. 'Can I help?'

He shook his head, already serving the fried food onto square white plates. 'No need. Table's laid, tea's made, food's cooked and the toast rack is full.' He held out a plate to her, smiling with more charm than she knew what to do with. '*Bon appetit.*'

'*Bon appetit,*' she repeated, sinking into her chair.

He was a very persuasive man, she was beginning to see. A people person, for sure. But there was more to him than mere superficial charm, she guessed. There was a private side to him she hadn't seen yet. And she'd liked to get to know *that* Gideon better.

They ate breakfast at the small table in the kitchen, music playing quietly in the background. She stole covert looks at Gideon from time to time. He looked much fresher than she felt, and had clearly showered recently, his dark hair still slightly damp, a healthy glow about him as he tucked into his hot breakfast and sipped tea from a generous mug. He had placed a mug of tea in front of her too, the pot made before she'd come downstairs, almost as though he had heard her getting dressed. Which was possible; it was quite a creaky old house. But hopefully not haunted. Not after her confused dreams last night...

As he finished his last strip of curly bacon, he glanced across at her thoughtfully, saying, 'I found something last night that you probably ought to see.'

'Last night?' This surprised her. 'But I thought you went to bed at the same time as me?'

'Yes, I did... But then I had a sudden memory and went searching.' Gideon looked almost guilty, fiddling with the cutlery he'd set across his plate on finishing. 'You remember how we talked about those letters and whether Cecily had ever replied to Franklin?'

'I'm unlikely to have forgotten, given it was only yesterday.'

'Quite.' He nodded, still not looking at her. 'Of course, as I told you last night, I knew there wouldn't be much point asking Franklin about those letters now. Not given the patchy state of his memory.'

'Definitely not,' she agreed, hurriedly popping the

last crispy whites of fried egg into her mouth and wondering where this was leading to.

'The thing is, as I told you, Franklin lived here for a while before going into care. And I still have the bulk of his possessions up in the room that he used. I recalled seeing a cache of personal letters in a small archive box of documents that I'd looked through when he went into care. You know, they always want birth certificates and so on.' He paused, taking a sip of tea. 'So, after you'd gone to bed last night, I went in there and did some rummaging.'

She stared at him, hastily swallowing her last morsel of food, her eyes wide with sudden apprehension. 'And? Did you find any letters from Cecily?'

'I certainly did.'

Penny gave a whoop of excitement. 'Oh, you star! But that's marvellous… When can we read them?' Seeing the tense set of his shoulders, her eyes narrowed on his face. Abruptly, she was suspicious that he knew something she didn't and was deliberately concealing it. 'Unless you've already read them?'

That was definitely guilt on his face. But why?

Gideon shrugged, not quite meeting her gaze. 'I did read through them, it's true. Though only briefly, as it was so late and I was tired. But, well, it's a bit awkward.'

She frowned. 'Meaning?'

'I know I should share her replies with you, as you shared his letters with me. But what would it achieve? I mean, it's all finished now, isn't it?' He turned his mug of tea around and around, staring into it almost glumly. 'Cecily unfortunately passed away and Franklin... He can barely remember his own name these days. So why rake over old history?'

Penny put down her own mug of tea, instantly alert. 'All right, what did you find out?' she demanded. 'Is it something bad?'

'I...' He glanced at her and away, his voice tailing off.

'You can't hide her letters from me. If Cecily wrote them, they belong to me, don't they?'

Now it was his turn to frown. 'How do you work that out?'

'My grandmother left everything to me, and those letters belonged to her. They're her copyright, even if she sent them to Franklin. So you can't keep them from me. It wouldn't be right.' She felt awkward, as though she were threatening him. Which she absolutely was not. Hurriedly, she softened her tone, adding, 'Please, Gideon, you must see that I have to read them too. We read Franklin's letters together. Now let's read Cecily's responses together. Okay?'

He met her gaze at last, and she saw the conflict in his gaze. What on earth were in those letters to make him want to suppress them too?

'Oh, very well,' he said with a muffled groan, and gulped at his tea. 'Though don't say later that I didn't warn you.'

Goodness, she thought, her heart thumping with surprise and uncertainty at this warning. How bad could Cecily's letters be? Whatever could he be trying to hide?

'Duly noted,' she said, and reached for his plate. 'Now, you made breakfast. So I should wash up.'

'You can't,' he said flatly.

She stared at him, on her way to the sink. 'Sorry?' Was he really so proprietorial about his kitchen that he couldn't bear to see anyone else armed with rubber gloves and a sponge?

'There's a dishwasher.' His wink reassured her. 'Just rinse them off and pop them in the machine. No need for extra labour.'

'Oh, I see.' Penny grinned. 'You had me going there.'

'Did I now?' Gideon stood, and she was struck again by how similar they were in height, his dark smiling eyes almost on a level with hers. 'That sounds promising, at least.'

She blushed.

Now what on earth had he meant by *that*?

CHAPTER SEVEN

Gideon was reluctant to sit down with this woman and discuss what he'd read in those letters last night. He had a strong suspicion she would become upset once she learnt what he'd discovered. However, before he could suggest that she took them away to look at on her own – the coward's way out, he admitted to himself, but less traumatic than having to see her face change as they were reading those letters together – he was saved by the bell. Literally, as his mobile rang.

Checking the number, he told her apologetically, 'It's work calling me. They only ring if it's an emergency. Do you mind if I take this?'

'Of course not.' Penny began to rinse off the plates in the sink, turning her back on him. He might not know her well, but he could tell that his reluctance had sown seeds of doubt in her mind about the treasure trove of letters. But he couldn't help it.

He liked her, that was the problem. And because he liked her, he couldn't bear the thought of seeing her hurt. Ridiculous, really. He had only just met the woman. But perhaps Franklin had been right all those years ago, when he was growing up and his godfather had warned him, 'You're too soft for your own good, my boy. Girls will take advantage of you. You need to harden up before someone makes you unhappy.'

Well, he had hardened up over the years. Mainly courtesy of several dead-end relationships that had left him shy of even making friends with women again. Indeed, the friendly approach always seemed to end in disaster. Maybe he *was* too soft. But right now, the important thing was to avoid hurting Penny, who had put much store by her unknown grandmother's love life and would be horribly disillusioned when she found out some of the facts surrounding that elderly lady's thought processes. Of course, the truth of those letters couldn't be hidden from her forever. But he still felt unprepared for the possibility that she might burst into tears...

Hurriedly, he stepped into the hall, closing the kitchen door behind him, and answered his mobile. 'Gideon here,' he said, and recognised the receptionist's voice on the other end. She sounded harassed. 'What's up, Sandra?'

'I'm really sorry, and I know it's your day off, and you haven't had a full day off work in ages, but –'

His mouth quirked in a wry smile. 'But something has come up. It's an emergency and I'm needed at the surgery. Am I close?'

'You're a mind reader. I don't know how you do it.'

Sandra's voice dripped with sarcasm.

'Give me the details.'

'Breech presentation up at Jolliet's dairy farm. The farmer needs you there straight away. Are you available?'

Gideon grimaced. Still, it was a useful excuse to avoid breaking the bad news to Penny.

'Unfortunately, yes. I'll be on my way in a few minutes.'

Ringing off, he headed back into the kitchen.

Penny had finished loading the dishes and cutlery in the dishwasher and was washing her hands at the sink. As he watched, she tutted under her breath and bent to place an errant fork in the cutlery section.

She had the cutest, curviest behind, he thought, eyeing it with interest, plus intriguingly long legs for a woman. For a few crazy seconds, he again entertained the possibility that she might be open to a relationship with him. Yes, he shouldn't have kissed her last night, and he had been careful not to show any overt sexual interest in her this morning, aware that he was slightly older than her and still pretty much a stranger. But he couldn't help himself.

She hadn't pushed him away last night, had she? And that unexpected impulse he'd felt as they said goodnight – to reach out and give her a kiss – was still very much alive. Her lips had tasted so good, and her body had felt so warm and sexy against his, it was hard not to repeat the experience. But he had a job to do, saving a cow in labour, not to mention her calf, and mooning over this young woman was hardly useful in the circumstances.

'I have to go, I'm afraid,' he admitted. 'Cow.'

She stiffened and paused in her hand-washing, looking round at him with an offended expression. 'Excuse me?'

'There's a cow in labour that needs a hand... Probably two.' He grimaced. 'Breech presentation.'

'Oh.' Her colour was heightened, but she was at least grinning. 'Sorry, I thought you were calling *me* a cow.' Her sudden chuckle was disarming. 'Look, a cow in labour sounds more urgent than my grandmother's letters. I'll get out of your hair and maybe we can meet up to discuss them later instead.' She dried her hands. 'How about tonight?'

Torn, he hesitated, his gaze on her face. *Of course* they should meet up. Yet he hated the thought of her reading those letters and what they contained...

'Actually,' he said slowly, 'I've changed my mind. I don't think it would be a good idea for me to share them with you.'

'What?' She looked taken aback.

'The thing is, there are some, erm, embarrassing things in them.'

'Embarrassing?'

She didn't seem to believe him. And she was right not to.

'Very,' he said, nodding sombrely. 'Things I'd rather not make public.'

'I won't tell a soul,' she promised him fervently, and he believed her. But that wasn't the point.

'I'm sure you wouldn't. But it's a privacy thing.' He

dug around for a better excuse. 'You see, I owe it to Franklin to keep those letters to myself. He's my godfather and I can't expose him to… to ridicule. Or people thinking poorly of him.'

Her eyes had widened, no doubt wondering what on earth he'd seen in Cecily's replies. 'I said I wouldn't breathe a word.'

'Well, you might forget and let something slip.'

'I'm sorry?'

Now she really was offended. And angry with him too. He saw the flash in her lovely blue eyes and regretted it. But anger was better than hurt and distress, wasn't it?

'I know it's not what you want but there it is.' He thrust his mobile into his pocket and opened the kitchen door so she could leave. 'Now, I'm really sorry, but I need to go right away, so… '

'So…what? *Get out*?'

He felt heat in his own face and knew he was being rude. But what choice did he have? 'Forgive me. I wish I could stand here and discuss the situation with you until you understood my reasoning. But that cow won't wait, I'm afraid. Every minute counts in a breech birth.'

Her expression changed and she nodded, moving past him swiftly to collect the tin of letters he'd left on the side after clearing up after last night. 'Of course. No, I'm the one who should be sorry. You must be keen to get going.' Hurrying to the front door with him following in her wake, she muttered, 'Thank you for last night's dinner… and breakfast…

and for sharing those letters with me.'

'You're welcome.' Grabbing up his emergency call-out kit bag from the porch, he added awkwardly, 'Last night was a real eye-opener.' He saw her sideways stare and managed a shrug. 'Goodbye.'

He locked up the house behind him, hearing her feet crunch away down the path. By the time he'd reached his car, Penny had gone.

Last night was a real eye-opener.

Why on earth had he said that? She must have thought he was being sarcastic. Or rude about her. Though in fact he had been perfectly serious, he realised. Meeting her and sharing those letters from the past had touched his heart. And almost nothing touched his heart these days, it had been frozen solid in his chest for so long…

The realization shocked him for a moment. Then he pulled out onto the busy street, heading off towards Jolliet's farm and focusing on the busy country lanes between there and town. He was struggling to get his head back into work mode. A cow in labour, having difficulties the farmer couldn't deal with. Two lives at stake. Time of the essence.

His painfully thawing heart would have to wait.

It was a few days later before Penny saw Gideon again. After the shock of having him refuse her access to her own grandmother's letters, she had stayed indoors at the flat and concentrated on clearing things out instead. It was a mammoth task and filthy too, with cobwebs and grim findings at the backs of the kitchen area cupboards, though she was disappointed not to have discovered any diaries or journals. That would have been useful, to hear Cecily's side. From the horse's mouth, as it were. Not that horses could speak, she ruminated.

She had however found a handful of letters from her grandfather, Peter.

He was presumably the same 'Peter' that Franklin had mentioned in his own correspondence as the reason he'd become jealous and gone off with Ophelia when they walked out as youngsters.

Unless Cecily had dated several Peters. Not inconceivable, but unlikely.

Her grandmother, to her surprise, appeared to have separated from Peter late on in their marriage, though it wasn't clear why.

Penny was dumbfounded on discovering this fact, having assumed the couple had been together until her grandfather's death about a decade ago.

Peter's own letters to Cecily were frustratingly short. Mere scribbled notes, really. But short as they were, they sounded bitter and accusing, and she wasn't sure what to make of them. The old phrase suggested that her grandfather had been unfaithful to Cecily. But without any real proof, Penny decided to reserve judgement. After all, given Franklin's cache of letters, and Gideon's bizarre refusal to let her see them, perhaps it had been the other way around.

That was a disturbing possibility but one she had

to face. Perhaps her grandmother had not been the saintly old lady she'd originally assumed her to be.

Talking of facing unpleasant things, early Monday morning, dragging two bulging binbags outside for the refuse collection, Penny came face-to-face with Gideon and stopped dead, staring.

Standing on the pavement opposite, her neighbour was also carrying a black bag for the binmen – though considerably smaller than her own – along with several containers of items for recycling. She had tried to sort out what rubbish in the flat could be recycled and what couldn't, but had given up on finding most of her grandmother's things were in serious disrepair.

'Hello,' Gideon said, dropping the recycling containers onto the curb with a clatter and looking back at her with a curious expression. Cars drifted past, but she barely noticed them, drawn to his face. 'I haven't seen you in a while. How have you been getting on?'

'Oh, um, you know…' She was still holding the binbags, she realised, hurriedly dumping them on the roadside like everyone else had done. 'Still plenty to do.'

They exchanged small talk about her work on the flat and the weather, while Penny wondered unhappily what exactly she had done to make him keep his distance. Perhaps offering to wash the breakfast dishes had been a step too far…

Then he said abruptly, 'Do you fancy coming over for a drink tonight?' She blinked, derailed from their nice cosy conversation about raincloud patterns. 'I've been thinking again about those letters your grandmother wrote and... Maybe I made the wrong decision.'

'Goodness.' Her heart skipped several beats. In fact, it took two strong gulps of diesel-laden breath from passing traffic to get it started again. 'Well, erm, that's very generous of you. If you're *sure*?'

'Seven o'clock,' he told her firmly.

Disconcerted by his smile, she muttered some nonsensical reply and hurried back inside, wishing she had at least tidied her hair into a ponytail and put clean jeans on that morning before venturing outside. The ones she was wearing were in desperate need of a closer acquaintance with the insides of a washing machine. But she hadn't been expecting to see her sexy neighbour on the other side of the road with his own rubbish, had she? Besides, since her gran's washer looked like something that had been phased out in the Fifties, and she had no clue where the nearest launderette was and not much money to spare on the expense of laundry anyway, clean clothes were at a premium right now.

The best she could do was shake the creases out of the last clean outfit in her rucksack and hope it passed muster for her date tonight.

A date?

Was it actually a date though, she wondered feverishly?

As in *a date*, date?

Or had Gideon merely asked her over for a drink

as a courtesy, because of the strange connection between them, this long-hidden cache of letters between Franklin and Cecily?

Whatever his motivation, she wasn't taking any chances. Before going over, she washed most body parts that needed it, double-brushed her teeth, dragged a comb through her blonde hair, and then stared at herself in the mirror in despair.

Who was she trying to kid?

She might own a flat and shop, courtesy of her gran, but until she decided to put it on the market, and it actually sold, which was by no means certain, given she had no idea of its soundness and viability as a building, she was a penniless nobody.

Why on earth would a totally together guy like Gideon even look twice at someone so lowly? Oh, maybe for a date or two. He had kissed her, after all. So there was attraction between them. But anything beyond a brief fling was highly unlikely. And she *liked* him, damn it. He was *a keeper*. She didn't want to start something with a man like him in a casual way and get her heart stomped on. That would be too awful.

'Tell me, what do you intend to do now?' Gideon asked, pouring her a glass of wine as they sat out in his lush, sunny, flower-filled back garden, which was idyllic, and made her yearn to stop living in that untidy little flat and get back on the road, where she could always sleep under the stars and feel the grass under her feet on waking. 'I mean, with the flat. You seem to have done a good job on clearing it up. Are you still planning to sell it?'

Penny glugged down some wine, willing herself to be strong. 'Actually, no.' She had been thinking about ever since seeing him earlier and had finally come to a decision. 'I'm going to try my hand at floristry.'

Gideon's eyebrows shot up and he choked on his wine. 'I… I beg your pardon?'

'I don't know much about being a florist, it's true… Nothing, in fact. Even my flower arranging skills are non-existent.' She swilled the wine round and round, staring into her glass rather than meeting his gaze. 'But I can learn, can't I? And I think I'd like to make a go of it, rather than simply sell up and pocket the cash. This will probably sound odd but I feel it's what Cecily would have wanted. Maybe even what she intended when she left it to me.' She saw his brows rise even further. 'Please don't ask me to explain how I know that. Because I can't. Only I feel it deeply. In here…' She tapped on her chest and saw his dark eyes follow the movement. Oh goodness! 'And here too.' Hurriedly, she tapped the side of her head. Which probably deserved to be drilled into in search of brains. 'Intuition, maybe.'

'I see.' There was a dry note to his voice but at least he didn't laugh. He put down his glass and flapped away an insect with his hand. His eyebrows were still raised, she noticed. Maybe they'd become permanently stuck in that elevated position. She imagined him trying to pull them down manually – maybe even enlisting her help in eradicating his perma-surprised look– and snorted into her wine glass, hurriedly turning that unladylike sound into throat-clearing at the last second. 'That's commendable. But won't you need capital for a venture like that? To buy stock and display units and... probably a new till?'

'Yes,' she agreed slowly. 'But I've unearthed a few treasures in the flat that might fetch enough to fund my first few weeks of stock and a few necessities. It wouldn't launch a big business. But I could try opening for the rest of the summer, at least. See how things go.'

He was frowning. 'What kind of *treasures*?'

'Book treasures.' She told him, as briefly as she could, that she had in fact discovered a chest of first editions of important botany books among her grandmother's possessions, some of them dating from the eighteenth century, hoarded by her grandmother. Even a cursory glance at online antiquarian bookshops had told her they could raise quite a tidy sum as a specialist collection. A small chest, it had been hidden away at the end of the bed under a heavy quilt, so no doubt others had missed it too when going through the flat's contents.

She felt uncomfortable selling anything her grandmother had so clearly treasured. But running the flower shop even for a few weeks would bring her closer to Cecily's everyday life than she could get simply by scanning letters, and that was the most important thing to focus on. Trying to *understand* her grandmother's life and ambitions.

'I've found a local dealer online who's agreed to come and value the books, and buy them on the spot if he's satisfied by their condition.'

'Well, good luck to you with that,' Gideon said and raised his glass. 'And congratulations. Here's to reopening the flower shop!'

'To the flower shop,' Penny murmured, clinking her glass against his. Catching his curious gaze on her face, which was more flushed than it ought to be in this late sunshine, she stirred restlessly. 'You told me you'd changed your mind about Cecily's replies to Franklin. But what does that mean in real terms?'

She paused, leaning back in her garden chair to gaze at him. Her heart was beating awfully fast, she thought, and blamed it on the wine and the heat of the summer evening.

'Does it mean you're planning to let me read her letters?'

CHAPTER EIGHT

'Of course.'

Gideon's heart was thumping like a drum. A drum being beaten by someone with an appalling sense of rhythm. Or perhaps a drunken drummer, missing beats and sometimes the whole drum altogether. Why he was getting so angsty about this, he couldn't fathom. It really wasn't his business. And yet...

'In fact, I came prepared.' He opened the folder he'd placed on the wicker garden table and passed her a small stack of letters. 'There you go.' His gaze held hers. 'Only don't shoot the messenger, okay?'

'I never shoot anyone if I can help it.'

'I mean it.' She had taken a grip on the letters, but he refused to let go of his end, still reluctant to do this to a girl he'd begun to really like. More than like, perhaps. 'Seriously, Penny... There are things in here that maybe you won't like.'

'I'll deal with it.'

His gaze clashed with hers briefly, and a frisson ran down his spine. 'Fine.' He released the letters, and she sank back, clutching them to her chest. 'Don't say I didn't warn you.'

'Obviously.' She opened the top letter eagerly and began to read silently. He saw a frown gather on her brows. Then darken and deepen. Like a gathering storm. She bit her lip, then swore under her breath. Then looked up at him with eyes already glistening with a hint of tears. 'Okay, you warned me.' She passed the letter back to him. 'Perhaps you could… read it aloud? From the middle… about *there*.' Her slender finger pointed.

'Me?' He felt his own brows soar.

'Easier than reading it to myself, trust me.' Her voice held a tremble. 'Please.'

Gideon took a deep breath, then nodded and began reading from where she'd pointed. It seemed he had a soft spot for this woman. Otherwise, he would have refused. Wouldn't he?

'*You wanted to know why I'm not in touch with my daughter anymore. I should have told you this before, but I didn't want you to feel guilty, because it was partly your fault. Years ago, she found out about you and me. That bit was my fault. I'd been reading your old letters to me from before Peter, and left them out on the kitchen table. She came in from work and found them. We had a blazing row. If you hadn't written such things to me – especially about her dad – she might not have packed a bag and stormed out. But that's families for you. Nobody ever expects a parent to have a complicated private life. And if they do, it's unforgiveable.*' His voice slowed and he shot a glance at Penny to see her crying soundlessly. The sight shook him. 'You want me to stop?' But she shook her head, and after a hesitation, he went on, feeling torn in two. *'She's had a child of her own now, so maybe she'll learn in time. But maybe not. She was never exactly an empathetic person. Her baby is a girl. I've not met her. Maybe I never will. But a friend in their area sent me a newspaper cutting from the birth announcement. I cried when I read it, it was so wonderful but also upsetting. Because she hasn't told me herself about the birth. Which means she hasn't forgiven me. That I'm still hated for having loved someone other than her blessed father. Of course, she asked the dreaded question when she found those letters. "Do you still love Franklin?" And I had to tell the truth. She burnt the letters and swore to my face that if she ever had children, she would erase me from history. I would never know them, and if I ever tried to find them, she would teach those children to hate me. So now you know why I must never, ever try to contact her. Because I don't want some innocent child suffering because of me.'*

He lowered the letter and risked another look at her face, which was ravaged with tears. 'I'm sorry. Though at least it shows she was thinking of you.'

'My mum though… What a hateful person.'

'You can't know that.'

'Did you hear what you were just reading? She blamed my gran for having been in love with two people at once, and burnt her first love letters from Franklin, and then left and never came back.'

Her voice was clogged with bitter tears. 'Then she pretended that my grandmother had died years ago. A total lie. She denied me the chance to meet Cecily. To get to know her while she was still alive.'

'Yes, that was pretty mean,' he admitted, and inwardly groaned at how pathetic that comment was, given the gravity of the situation. But what else could he say?

Luckily, she hadn't noted the rubbish support he was offering, going on tearfully, 'But Cecily clearly still wanted to know me. That's why she left me the flat... and the letters. She wanted me to know about all this.' She waved a hand at the letters and then ran a hand over wet eyes. 'Oh God, it's too awful. Poor poor Gran.'

He couldn't help himself but dropped the letter and jumped up, hurrying around to put an arm about her. 'Hey, hey,' he murmured, squeezing her awkwardly. 'It was all a long time ago... There's no need to be so sad.'

'I'm not sad,' she said through gritted teeth, still sobbing. 'I'm... angry.'

He released her. 'Oh.'

'This is... anger. At my mum, mostly. But also at the universe. For letting bad things happen to good people.'

He sank down in a crouch beside her, wishing he could understand this rare, complicated, possibly deranged woman better. 'So this is anger? You're channelling rage here?'

'Ye-ssss,' she hissed, scrubbing at her eyes now

with undiluted fury.

'Okay.' Loving her spirit, he dared to smile, though ready to retreat in a hurry if she smacked him around the head. 'Good to know. And what does sadness look like?'

'Oh… trust me, you'll know when you see it.' Penny bent her head forward, hiding her face in her hands for a moment. Then grabbed a huge lungful of air and threw her head back violently, making him glad he hadn't still been hugging her, as she might have dislocated his shoulder with that power move. 'Right.'

His eyes narrowed on her flushed profile. 'Right?'

'No more tears.' She grabbed at the letters so clumsily they scattered over the grass, and she bent to pick them up. 'Damn it… Sorry.'

He stooped to help and their heads collided with a distinct crack. Pain flashed through him. 'Ouch!'

'Ouch!' she yelped too.

They laughed at the same time, both also groaning afterwards in unison, clutching their aching foreheads.

The smile in his heart grew. 'Penny,' he began, meaning to ask if he could kiss her again, but she interrupted him.

'I have an idea,' she said determinedly.

Taking a deep breath, he pushed the question to the back of his head. It could wait. By the look in her eyes, this was more important.

'Go on.'

'In Franklin's letters, he mentioned places where

the two of them met for dates... Well, for drinks or a walk or just a chat, I suppose. But they were really dates, weren't they?'

He studied her face, captivated by the glow in her eyes. 'Erm, I guess.'

'I'd like to reenact those dates.'

He blinked, taken off guard. 'I beg your pardon?'

'Let's go on those dates... You and me. The same dates they went on in and around Merriweather.' She seized his hand, her stare intense and emotional. A bit too emotional for his nerves to cope with. 'As an homage to Cecily and Franklin. And to spite my mum, who clearly made poor Gran miserable in her later years by keeping me away from her. Let's do it for them.'

As Gideon straightened, she released his hand. He was smiling but alarm bells were ringing inside him. A kiss was one thing. But – and here he returned to his previous fears – a date, and indeed numerous dates, were something very different.

Dates meant 'serious'.

And he wasn't sure about 'serious'.

What did he have to offer any woman, after all? He lived for his work, or always had so far. A woman in his life on a permanent or even semi-permanent basis would only lead to heartache for both of them.

He put a hand back to his still throbbing head. 'Um, I'm not sure.

'Oh, come on!' Penny waved the letters at him. 'Where's the harm?' Her voice had turned persuasive, though he could still hear that slight tremble that told him how much this meant to her. 'Look, I'll pay… Once I've got the cash for those valuable first editions, that is. You won't end up out of pocket.'

Gideon ran a hand through his hair, frowning. 'It's not the money.'

'Then what?'

He met her gaze, conflicted. How could he explain without leaving his own feeling and vulnerabilities wide open? And equally how could he disappoint her by refusing?

'Erm, never mind. Hang on, let me think…'

He sank back into the garden chair beside her. Trees rustled in the breeze, and the fragrance of summer flowers filled the air. He was reminded of Cecily's shop. His godfather had taken him there quite frequently as a boy, and he had loved the rich exotic scents of flowers whenever they walked through the shop door, and Cecily's warm smile, welcoming both him and Franklin. He missed her, he realised with a shock. And his childhood. He missed that too.

'Yes, all right, why not?' He forced a cheerful smile to his lips, giving her what he hoped was a decisive nod. 'It does sound like a lovely idea. Though I can't recall all the places where –'

'Oh, I've made a list,' she told him, and rummaged in her bag for it. He could see she looked strengthened by his agreement, and that at least felt good. 'How about the local pub first? That's easy enough. Then there's the woods on the edge of town where they went for a ramble. Deep and dark and very Cornish, those woods. I've seen website photos. And apparently there's good parking. So we could take your car and wouldn't have to walk.' She smiled, oblivious to his disquiet at this suggestion, carefully rechecking her list. 'Oh yes, and once they went to the seaside for the day. Fish and chip dinner followed by ice cream,' she reminded him helpfully, 'plus a long walk along the promenade.'

'Ah yes, their seaside date.' This was not going to end well, he thought gloomily, but kept smiling. 'How could I have forgotten?'

The pub date was his first indication that his instincts about her had been right. He was very much in danger of making a fool of himself over this woman. They sat in the backroom snug, him cradling a pint, her nursing a bitter shandy – apparently her grandmother's preferred drink – and chatted awkwardly about the small town of Merriweather and its history. She had found a few histories of the town in the flat and produced them, the two of them poring over replicas of medieval maps and sidebars discussing sheep pens and a sixteenth century livestock market where the supermarket now stood. He had expected to be bored when she took these out, but in fact had enjoyed the evening thoroughly.

After a couple of drinks each, they had strolled back along the High Street and imagined the medieval town there instead, with Penny even pointing out old stones used in local buildings that might have dated from that period. The church was of later early Victorian construction, the original on another site having long since disappeared, but she had a few choice anecdotes about a series of naughty Victorian vicars whose antics had shocked the good townsfolk of Merriweather.

He'd thrown back his head and laughed, genuinely amused, and then found it too hard to say goodnight to her as they stood on opposite sides of the road in the dusk, so just kept her chatting as traffic gently rumbled past.

She seemed keener than him to get home. Which worried Gideon that he was falling for someone who didn't feel the same way. But then she would smile and he'd feel it had to be impossible for someone to smile at him like that – like the sun coming out – and *not* feel the same helpless yearning he was experiencing inside.

'Until next time,' Penny told him airily for the third time, waving.

'The woods?'

'The woods.' She pointed towards his car, parked on the drive behind him. Maybe she'd picked up his hesitation with her special emotion antennae because she frowned and added, 'It's only five minutes' drive outside town. You're up for that, surely?'

'Of course.'

But inwardly he was remembering a time when, as a young man, he'd taken a previous girlfriend to the woods late at night and parked up for a kiss and cuddle. That had not gone well. Though his kissing technique was better these days. But the woods still brought back bad memories. And it would be a strangely intimate space, especially on a warm summer's evening like tonight.

'We don't have to stay long,' she said. 'If you're not keen.'

He was making *her* nervous, he realised, and instantly felt guilty. 'No, let's do this properly or not at all. They went for a ramble, yes?'

'A walk or ramble, yes. With a picnic. On a Saturday afternoon.'

'Then let's commit to doing the same.' What was wrong with him? A girlfriend was the last thing he needed. Yet here he was encouraging her to pursue this crazy path. 'Saturday afternoon? Unless it's raining?'

'I'm praying for sunshine.'

'Not too much sunshine. I burn easily.'

'I'll bring sunscreen. And a parasol. And gender-neutral sunhats.' She winked.

He grinned, sinking his hands in his pockets. Her humour was infectious. 'You're on. Make mine a yellow sunhat. I like yellow. Sunshine yellow.'

'I prefer blue. Sky blue.'

'The two of us will be like the sun in the heavens.'

'Or a banana in a swimming pool.'

He gave a bark of laughter, backing away slowly. 'You're good at that, you know.'

'Ridiculous imagery?'

'Capping my jokes.'

'I guess we make an excellent double act.' Her gaze held his, eyes twinkling. 'Until next time, then.'

He wanted to dash across the road in front of traffic and kiss her.

But that would be stupid.

Not least because there was a local bus coming, churning up the dust, and those council-run buses stopped for nobody. Sometimes not even people waiting at the bus stop.

'Next time,' he agreed.

But he waited until Penny had gone inside the flower shop before he trailed up the path into his own home, feeling oddly flat now their first 'date' was over.

She had sold those valuable books, she'd told him in the pub, and had begun restocking the flower shop. There was a handwritten banner in the freshly cleaned window that read: GRAND REOPENING NEXT WEEK. And beyond it he could see vases on the display units, and a till on the counter, and brightly painted walls.

It made him feel good to imagine walking in through that door with Franklin on his arm again, just as they'd done all those years ago, to smell the gorgeous flowers and see the welcoming smell of a beautiful lady behind the counter…

Maybe he did understand why Franklin had waited so patiently for Cecily. Why he'd never given up, even as the decades passed and there seemed no point. Why he'd stayed true to his wife, like the man of honour he was, yet still never forgot the woman he'd loved first and stupidly abandoned.

Because there was no telling the heart to be silent. Not when it was leaping and thumping and clamouring for love.

CHAPTER NINE

Penny knew that it was crazy to be yearning for a man who was so clearly out of reach, being solvent, dependable, settled... All the things she wasn't and never had been. And even if he hadn't been out of reach, she could see that he wasn't interested in pursuing a relationship. Everything about Gideon had shouted no commitment from the start. And she respected that.

She had never been particularly interested in a committed relationship either; she enjoyed her freedom as a single person far too much.

Commitment meant the end of freedom, so it was something she'd always avoided like the plague. (Though the comparison wasn't quite right, was it? Commitment didn't bring you out in sweaty boils in your armpits or leave you to die a horrible pustule-covered death in some medieval hell-hole, like the plague did. Though maybe it might *feel* like that at times...) There was also the fact that she had little experience of commitment, except for seeing her father and stepmother forced to live together far from blissfully. And that relationship would be enough to put even the most romantic soul off the idea of marriage.

Yet here she was, walking along a woodland path with a man she increasingly saw as her 'boyfriend' – at least, he was male and a friend – a rucksack on her back filled with lunch items and the bottle of bubbly that he had provided, for the 'romantic' picnic they had planned. They had plastic glasses for the wine, and chicken drumsticks, and a large bag of pretzels. And a folded square of checked fabric to sit on, in case of ants or damp grass. Though it had been so sunny for days now, the woodland path was dry as dust and the sun beat down on their yellow and blue sun hats as though this were the Mediterranean, not Cornwall.

They really ought to be at the seaside on a gorgeous sunny day like this.

But the seaside trip was slated to be their third date. Or rather, the third reenactment of Franklin and Cecily's dates. Not a *real* date, she had to remind herself.

Part of her wanted to be honest with him, and say straight out, 'I fancy the pants off you, Gideon. Let's get together.' But another part of her was so terrified by that prospect that she felt her throat close up every time her mouth opened, in case those words came out by accident and she couldn't take them back.

Yet what was she really scared of? That he would

say no?

She had a sneaking suspicion he might actually say yes to a relationship. And maybe that was the most terrifying thing of all. That Gideon's overt fear of commitment would not prevent him from indulging in a romantic fling. They would date for real, then. Kisses and everything. With a heavy emphasis on the *everything* part.

But it wouldn't last long. Maybe a few half-hearted dates before he grew tired of the game and broke up with her. And that would be awful. Heartrending and embarrassing too. They would still be living opposite each other in town, but never speaking.

Surely friendship was better than silence?

'Phew,' he said, glancing at her as he ran a hand across his forehead, 'it's so hot today. I bet we get a few animals being brought into the surgery this evening, sick from too much heat or not enough water.'

She stared at him. 'Does that really happen?'

'I'm afraid so.' His dark, lean face grew sombre. 'Sadly, despite all the public information warnings, some people *still* leave their dogs in their cars while they go shopping or to the pub for hours. And in hot weather like this, sometimes those animals will die.'

'Oh my God, that's horrible.' Penny shuddered. 'I've heard of that happening. But to see it first-hand… That must be awful for you.'

'Yes,' he said briefly, staring ahead, walking with hands in his pockets. 'I probably ought to be used to it by now. I mean, we often have to put animals down at the surgery. When they're very sick or there's no hope of a recovery from an injury, you know? It's always terribly sad. But to see a healthy animal who died simply because their owner didn't let them out of a boiling hot vehicle...' His voice choked and tailed off into silence as his face grew shuttered and grim. 'Sorry. I'm spoiling the day. Let's talk about something else.'

'Of course.'

Penny loved how sensitive he was, not only to the plight of the animals in his care but to her own feelings. He was a genuinely nice person. And she had met so few of them in her life.

She herself was not nice. She could only aspire to niceness. Not that she was a *viper*. But she often harboured dark thoughts about other people, and she guessed that Gideon never harboured anything, let alone dark thoughts. He was too straightforward and pleasant, though the darkness in his eyes just now when he'd spoken of suffering animals had indicated a more complex side to his nature too, and she loved that about him.

It meant his feelings ran deep – and that could never be a bad thing in a man.

Most of the men she'd dated over the years had been about as shallow as muddy streams or even puddles. In comparison to their lack of emotional depth, Gideon was the Atlantic Ocean. Deep and mysterious, or so it seemed to her some days, wandering along Merriweather's coastal paths, and staring out across the blue-grey ocean. How marvellous it was, she thought, to live in this beautiful Duchy of Cornwall, to see the ocean roll majestically past every day and stare out over fields and lush green hills, growing mistier and mistier in the distance, and know that she had come home here. Home to her true family, to where her grandmother had lived and worked for years.

It made her feel grounded to be here in Cornwall. She had never felt grounded or 'at home' before in her entire life. And much of that had to be down to learning about Cecily and Franklin.

Home is where the heart is. That's what people said, wasn't it?

And her heart was definitely *here*.

'What are you thinking?' Gideon asked abruptly, his voice deep. He had stopped ahead of her on the woodland path, his brows tugging together in a frown. 'Did I upset you just now? If so, I'm sorry. I didn't mean to.'

There was nobody else in sight. The moment felt quiet and intimate. So quiet that she could hear the rapid thump of her heart.

'No,' she said, wishing she could tell him the truth, but aware that could be disastrous. 'I was just thinking what a nice man you are.' She almost groaned out loud at how lame that sounded. Birds twittered above them in the trees, the sun striking through the leafy branches, as she stopped to look at him apologetically. 'That is to say, you're just so…' She struggled for the right word but couldn't find one that would both describe him accurately and not make her sound like a love-addled fool. 'Well, *nice*.'

Gideon said nothing for a moment, staring back at her. A muscle jerked in his jaw. '*Nice*?' He looked away as though disgusted with what she'd said. At least, that was the expression on his face. 'Thanks a bunch,' he drawled. 'That's great to hear. But *nice* wasn't what I was aiming for.'

'Sorry.' Penny grimaced, putting a conciliatory hand on his arm. Good grief, his muscles were impressive. 'I honestly didn't mean it in a bad way.'

The truth was, he wasn't *nice*. He was wildly, gobsmackingly amazing. But she could hardly have said that, could she? Or not without exposing her own feelings.

His head turned back towards her, his gaze dropping to the hand on his arm. '*Nice*,' he repeated in the same slightly bitter tone, this time drawing out the long syllable. Was that irony in his voice? 'Oh, that's marvellous.'

She hated the idea that she had hurt his feelings by trying so clumsily to compliment him. It gnawed at her insides.

Daringly, she moved a little closer. Close enough that she could smell his citrus aftershave and see lighter hazel flecks in his dark eyes. 'Gideon…' she began huskily, meeting his gaze, but got no further.

'I'll show you how nice I am,' he muttered.

His other arm came around her, drawing her close, and his head approached hers, though this time less precipitously than when they had bumped foreheads in the garden. But it was just as shocking when their lips met and she gasped against his mouth, seized by the most delicious sensations that her head actually *swam*.

Oh goodness!

His strong arms held her tight and she let the kiss go on, her eyes firmly closed – both against the bright dappled sunlight in the woods and against reality, knowing this was such a huge mistake – willing it never to end.

But of course it did end.

And with a bump.

'Good Lord!' a stern female voice exclaimed, mere feet away from them. 'Gideon?' Then, when Gideon did not instantly release her but merely stiffened – not like *that*! she batted the scandalous thought away with a rush of heat to her cheeks – there was an embarrassed clearing of the throat, and the voice added more delicately, 'Erm... children present, Gideon. Maybe time to cease and desist?'

At once, Gideon's arms fell away, and he and she both turned in blinking astonishment to discover the source of this interruption.

Now Penny's face flared with genuine heat, and her hands flew to her cheeks, mortified at the sight of a small group of ramblers staring at them on the woodland path.

Sure enough, there were young children among the group, plus several mild-faced elders in sunhats and with walking sticks, and – surely the worst cut of all – a lady vicar, in full dog collar get-up, her disapproving eyes bulging as she surveyed the two miscreants she'd discovered 'making out' in the woods. One of the old ladies tut-tutted, a small boy chuckled and ran about waving his hands, and a heavy-set gentleman in shorts with pasty white legs made an off-colour remark that had Gideon's jaw clenching with immediate belligerence.

'Whatever are you doing, Gideon?' the vicar demanded, shooing her group of walkers past them on the narrow path. 'And who is this?'

It was on the tip of Penny's tongue to say, 'None of your business!' but she painfully bit said tongue, and tidied her hair and clothing instead of being offensive. Not that she was particularly mussed up after 'The Kiss' but the vicar's sharp eyes had made her feel as though the two of them had been rolling about half-naked in the shrubbery, not exchanging a quick and meaningless kiss between friends.

A quick and meaningless kiss?
Between friends?

Who on earth was she gaslighting, other than herself? Astonished by her own stubborn obtuseness, Penny rolled her eyes internally – doing so externally would have been weird and probably insulted the vicar even further – and made a mental note to stop fooling herself when it came to her feelings for this man.

She fancied Gideon madly, and liked him far more than was good for her sanity, and had in fact been longing for him to roll her into the shrubbery for more kissing (and possibly other forms of strenuously expressed affection too).

Meanwhile, he was talking to the vicar in a tightly controlled manner, though his own colour was heightened and his fists were clenched. 'This is Penny,' he was saying, not meeting Penny's eyes, 'who's just inherited the old florist's shop in the High Street. She's Cecily's granddaughter.' He coughed. 'And a friend of mine.'

So they *were* friends, Penny thought, mentally poking herself with a sharp stick. As far as the vicar was concerned, at any rate.

The vicar thrust out a hand and Penny found herself forced to shake it or look rude. The woman's palm was sweaty, but her grip was firm. Almost violently so.

'Pleased to meet you,' the vicar said with an energetic nod. 'I'm Patsy. The local Rev.' She glanced between the two of them. 'I did see that the flower shop was being reopened. So that's your doing?' She paused. 'I haven't seen you about town. Been here long?'

'Not really. I only moved in a few weeks ago.'

'Only a few weeks, you say?' Patsy pursed her lips, her gaze shooting to Gideon's face. 'So, did you two, erm, know each other previously?'

'Yes,' Gideon said.

'No,' Penny said simultaneously.

Gideon's fulminating glance met hers and she blenched.

'I m-mean, yes,' she stammered.

'I mean, no,' Gideon also said at the same time, and

then flashed her another vengeful look. 'That is, sort of. In a manner of speaking.'

'I see,' Patsy said drily.

'Erm, out with the flock today?' Gideon asked hurriedly, glancing after the walkers now some way along the path ahead of them.

'Walking the parish boundary,' the vicar explained briefly. 'We do it most years, but don't usually expect to be confronted with canoodling couples in the woods.' With a sniff, she added, 'Better take it indoors, Gideon. To avoid being the subject of local gossip.' With a surprising smile, she nodded to Penny. 'Again, nice to meet you, Penny. Maybe see you in church?'

At this, Penny was flooded with toe-curling embarrassment, not being much of a believer. But how to say that to *a vicar*, of all people, without causing offence?

'Oh, I… I'm not really…erm…'

'Maybe the two of you could come together one Sunday? Or a month of Sundays, in fact.' The vicar set off after her rapidly vanishing parishioners, loping along at an impressive pace and calling back over her shoulder, 'We offer church weddings at a reduced rate for regular attendees, you know.'

And on that enigmatic note, she was gone.

Penny closed her eyes, unable to face the man now groaning under his breath beside her. 'Well, that was… awkward.'

'My fault,' he said heavily.

She opened her eyes again and fixed him with a

hard stare. 'Yes.'

His eyebrows rose. 'I don't recall you fighting me off.'

'That's because I'm too polite for my own good.'

Again, those dark brows seemed stuck in position, high on his forehead. 'You're saying I kissed you against your will?'

'I'm saying… ' Suddenly deflated, Penny shook her head. 'No, I kissed you back.'

'Thank you.'

'But what just happened… That was very embarrassing.'

'We were seen drinking together at the pub,' he pointed out, watching her with curious eyes. 'You didn't seem to mind that.'

'Having a drink together is innocent enough. But that… the kissing thing…' Her cheeks flared again as she recalled how tightly he'd held her. And how she'd hoped he would go further. 'That wasn't innocent.'

'No,' he agreed.

'And now the vicar thinks…'

'Yes.'

'And all those other people too.'

'Yes.'

She buried her hot face in her hands. 'I didn't want to be the subject of gossip.'

'Me neither.'

'I hate being talked about. It's one of the worst things ever.'

'I'm with you on that.'

'Yes, but men... You can get away with kissing people left, right and centre.'

'We can?' His eyebrows soared again.

'Without attracting censure, yes.'

He stuck his hands in his pockets and studied her face, suddenly sombre. 'You feel censured by what just happened?'

'I feel...' She let out an exasperated breath. 'Silly and embarrassed, and like people are going to point at me next time I walk down the High Street.'

'They won't.'

'I feel like I want to hide out in that flower shop until the end of my days.'

'That would be a shame.' When she moved to walk back to the car, her cheeks flaming, he took her hands and stopped her. 'Hang on, I want to say...'

'Yes?' she demanded.

'I'm sorry,' he said, and held her gaze. 'And that was incredible.'

Opening her mouth to rail at him again, Penny closed it and swallowed hard. Incredible? What was he talking about, exactly?

'Do you mean, the bit where...' She flapped a hand uncertainly. 'The bit where the vicar saw us and all the people –'

'I mean, the kiss.'

'Oh.'

'And I'd like to do it again. With your permission.'

Now she couldn't even say, 'Oh,' but mouthed it anyway, her eyes raised mutely to his. His hands drew her closer.

'Do I have it?' he murmured.

'What?' She felt dazed, wondering if he'd always been this staggeringly handsome or had suddenly become a Greek god in just the last few seconds.

'Your permission to kiss you again. Do I have it?'

She sucked in a breath. Because it was always hard to breathe when he kissed her, she was discovering, and it might be wise to have some air in her lungs before they started again.

'But what about gossip... The vicar may come back.'

'She won't. They're walking the bounds. One way only.'

'Oh... Right, yes.'

'Was that yes, I have your permission?' He smiled into her eyes, sending her pulse racing. 'Or yes, the vicar won't be back.'

She gave a shy smile in return, her heart flooding with warmth. 'Both,' she whispered, and let him pull her into his arms.

CHAPTER TEN

Within forty-eight hours of being discovered kissing in the local woods, it seemed everybody in Merriweather knew that he and Penny were an item.

As in, *everybody*. From the paper boy to the bus driver to the poodle-owning woman in the supermarket who had given Gideon a knowing grin as they exchanged their usual friendly, 'Good morning,' in the checkout queue. *She* knew. *The paper boy* knew. And so did *the bus driver*, surely, who could have had no other reason for the inexplicable thumbs-up he'd given Gideon in passing.

He dreaded going into work.

Eventually though, he couldn't put off the evil moment any longer. Sandra was on the phone when he walked in – she was always on the phone; in fact, he suspected she'd had it surgically grafted to her ear – but she stopped speaking long enough to lean forward through the glass partition and say with a wink, 'Good weekend, Gideon? Do anything fun? With anyone interesting? As if I need ask...'

Horrified, he fled to the prep area to scrub up and put on his PPE, then slipped into the sanctuary of his examination room, where he was soon joined by Mrs James and an overweight boxer. (Not a prize fighter in need of shedding a few pounds, but a much beloved family pet.)

The boxer, whose name was Daisy, had been suffering from bloat, a common condition in that breed.

'Is her condition no better, Mrs James?' he asked, examining the dog, who stood unhappily but without growling, peering up at him as he palpated her stomach. 'Have you tried spreading out her meals during the day? Lots of smaller meals rather than one big one? And the dietary changes I recommended last time?'

'I've followed your instructions to the letter,' the owner told him, patting Daisy's head soothingly to keep her docile. 'It's my husband, you see. He won't stop slipping her tidbits. Unhealthy stuff too. Bacon, crisps, leftover chips… He's a menace.'

'I think an X-ray might be in order. To check what's going on inside her. If you could bring Daisy back after morning surgery, say around two o'clock, I'll organize that for you.' As he was stripping off his gloves, Gideon caught her curious glance on his face and asked, 'Something else bothering you?'

'Nothing, no.' Mrs James gave a nervous laugh, adding, 'It's just… Well, I heard you were courting at last.'

'Courting?'

'Going out with a girl. That woman who's reopening the flower shop. None of my business, of course. But I just wanted to wish you both well and say, it's about time.'

'I'm sorry?' He felt his stomach clench.

'You've been single ever so long. A lovely man like you… It's a shame. Though my husband's always said –' Her voice tailed off into an awkward silence.

Gideon knew he shouldn't ask. Yet couldn't help himself. 'Go on, don't stop there. What's your husband always said?'

'Well, not just him but everyone. We've always wondered if you actually… Whether you prefer…' She stopped again, looking acutely embarrassed.

'Men?'

'Animals.' Her cheeks flamed and she bit her lip, her agonized gaze shooting to the boxer, who whined in a disconsolate fashion. 'Oh, not in *that* way. Goodness, no. Ha ha.' Her voice had become high-pitched, and she was looking flustered. 'I just meant… We all thought you were married to your work, that's all.'

'I see.' Gideon folded his arms.

'I do hope I haven't offended you. Come along, Daisy.' Mrs James led her boxer from the room, smiling back at him over her shoulder. The overweight dog waddled after her with its classic wide-legged, broad-chested boxer gait. 'Anyway, we're all hoping it works out for you. You deserve to be happy.'

'I do?'

'Oh yes,' she said blithely. 'You're ever such a *nice* young man.'

As the door swung shut behind her, Gideon resisted the urge to throw his box of sterile blue gloves at the wall. There was that word again. *Nice*.

Growing up, he'd always wanted to be considered magnetic, dangerous, charismatic. Those were the men who got the girls.

Instead, it seemed he was simply *nice*.

And he was definitely not *young* anymore, either. Training to be a veterinary surgeon had cost him many years of study, and there was a small but possibly significant age difference between him and Penny. Stupid, perhaps, but he feared being older than her might count against him.

Things had progressed between them, yes. Penny had let him kiss her several times now. But she had not yet set a time for their final Cecily and Franklin 'reenactment' date – a walk along the promenade, with seaside fish and chips and ice cream – which made him worry she might have changed her mind about their 'friendship'. Maybe the embarrassment of being spotted in his arms in public had put her off the whole idea. Or maybe she'd been ribbed by a few locals too about their relationship, and had decided to nip things in the bud before he got any ideas about future kisses.

The thought that she might be about to dump him was enough to make him wish to sink under the floorboards. But there were still sick, hurt and nervous pets out there waiting for his attention, and he had no time for self-pity. This was his job and he needed to do it, regardless of his fears and the awkward jokes everyone kept making about him and Penny. If she never went out with him again, he would still have his work, after all. He would still have all his feathered and furred friends. And some of the prickly ones too, from his seasonal work rescuing and treating injured hedgehogs. And then there was Toad Watch....

Though he knew his abiding love of and fascination for birds, mammals and amphibians was hardly a substitute for the euphoria he felt in Penny's company. That euphoria seemed to be highly addictive too, for he couldn't stop wondering how soon he could see her again and feel that soaring joy in his heart...

But how did Penny feel about *him*?

He suspected he knew the answer to that one, and it wasn't particularly gratifying.

Nice.

Gideon groaned.

Closing his eyes, he counted slowly to ten, then put on a brave smile and strode out to help old Mr Fairfax into the examination room with his feral tabby.

The little old flower shop was awash with the richest, sweetest floral fragrance and the most intensely coloured, eye-catching blooms and seed heads. The front windows had been cleaned and polished inside and out, the shop floor swept and mopped, the counters were gleaming, and the display vases looked so lovely, Penny thought her heart would burst with pride as she stood in the middle of the shop and turned on her heel, looking around at everything she had done to bring Cecily's disused shop back to life. Up in the flat, she'd found a few paper clippings about the flower shop, plus some faded photographs of Cecily herself behind the counter, and had tried to replicate the layout as closely as possible.

Cecily's framed photograph of herself with Franklin stood right next to the till, while other old photos of Cecily had been blown up and placed on the walls around the shop.

'Stunning,' a voice said from the doorway, and she turned, her heart leaping in surprise at the sight of Gideon standing there, arms folded, looking madly dishy in a white, open-necked shirt with both sleeves rolled up to the elbow and tight-fitting black jeans. 'It's just how I remember it when I was a boy. That amazing smell...' He straightened up, taking a deep breath of the flower-fragrant air, and his eyes closed briefly. 'Yes... I can almost see Cecily standing there, just like she used to, welcoming in her customers with that incredible smile that made everyone feel special.' He came into the shop, looking around, seeming to drink in every tiny detail. 'You've done a marvellous reconstruction job here.'

'Thank you,' she said huskily.

'When do you open for business?'

She checked her watch. 'About half an hour. I've

got the mayoress coming to cut a ribbon at ten o'clock, and the local paper is sending someone with a camera and to ask a few questions, and I'm hoping a few other people may turn up. I've been putting up leaflets for days and telling everyone I see, so fingers crossed, I won't be standing here on my lonesome all morning.' Though secretly she feared she might be.

'I'm sure you'll get a good crowd,' he said soothingly, and paused, his gaze on her face. 'Including my godfather, in fact.'

'Franklin's coming too? So he's feeling better, I take it?' When he nodded, she felt tears prick at her eyes and sucked in a shaky breath. 'Oh, thank you… That's wonderful news. I wasn't sure he'd be well enough.' Franklin had been suffering from a summer cold lately and she'd been steeling herself for the possibility that Cecily's old flame might not be able to make the grand reopening. 'It wouldn't have been the same without him here.'

'I know, and I told him so whenever I saw him and reminded him that the shop was reopening. The news seemed to help him get over his cold quicker. Though the way his memory is… I'm not sure he always understood what I was saying.'

'Poor thing.'

'It's very sad. He's getting worse. But he seems happy enough still. So that's something, I suppose.' He came closer. His clever eyes had narrowed on her face, and Penny felt suddenly nervous under so much intense scrutiny. 'I haven't seen much of you lately. Not since…' He stopped, looking away.

'Not since our woodland walk,' she finished for him, nodding awkwardly. She found herself wringing her hands. 'Yes, I ought to have called or texted you. The thing is, I've been madly busy with all this.'

'Of course.'

'I really *wanted* to speak to you.'

'Of course you did.'

She glared at him, frustrated, aware of an ironic gleam in those dark eyes. 'Yes, I honestly did. But there's been so much work involved in getting the shop ready.'

'And not a moment of it wasted.' He looked about at the pretty bouquets and floral arrangements and a vase of stunning arum lilies peeping out from twists of gold foil paper. He smiled, though his expression struck her as somehow sad. 'It's a triumph.'

'I hope everyone thinks so.' She paused. 'Especially Franklin. In a way, I've done it for him as much as for Cecily.'

'It's much appreciated, trust me,' he told her sincerely. 'I couldn't have found anything myself that would make him as happy as stepping back into this shop will, with all its wonderful sights and smells... You're recreated his past here, Penny, and I thank you for it.'

Her heart flooded with joy at his words, though she noticed that he didn't close the gap between them and try to kiss her again, almost as though he'd grown tired of her and their brief dating 'game'. This thought abruptly depressed her and she had to force a smile to her lips, all her joy draining away as she considered how it would feel to keep seeing him about the town but never being able to kiss him or feel his arms about her again…

Perhaps she ought not to have held off from contacting him for so long. But he hadn't contacted her, had he? So they were both to blame.

And she barely knew him.

Perhaps this kind of on-off behaviour was normal for him.

She didn't believe that though.

He had the kindest eyes.

'People have been gossiping about us,' she burst out.

His smile died. 'I know, and I'm sorry.'

'I thought I was imagining it at first. The stares and whispers… Then the librarian Tracy – your know Tracey, the redhead? – she asked me if it was true that I was dating the vet, and I… I…' Her face burnt with embarrassment and she couldn't go on. She had told the woman a stern, uncategorical no, of course. What else could she have said? They *weren't* dating, after all. But it had cost her dear to admit that. Because she sorely wished they *were*.

Gideon swore under his breath, apologised for his bad language, shuffled his feet, and then thrust his hands into his pockets, his air savage. 'Sorry,' he muttered, 'but I have no idea why so many people in this town think it's okay to gossip about people and ask such rude questions, to poke their noses in where –'

'Oh no.' She rushed to interrupt him, not wanting him to go off and corner the unfortunate librarian about her probing questions. 'I'm sure Tracey was just being curious.'

'They're all "just being curious". Curiosity doesn't give them the right to embarrass other people and make them unhappy.'

'I know. But the gossip will die down eventually.' She smiled bravely. 'All we have to do is wait.'

He looked at her searchingly. 'Is it?'

'Yes.' She shrugged, feeling herself on uncertain ground. 'Why, what were you thinking?'

'We never went on that third date.'

'The seaside walk?'

'Fish and chip supper,' he agreed.

'And ice cream afterwards.'

'We couldn't forget the ice cream. I wonder what flavour they ate on that date. Chocolate or vanilla? Or maybe strawberry?'

'We should ask Franklin.'

His smile vanished again. 'Would he remember, though?'

'You never know,' she said softly. 'Old memories are the last to fade, they say.'

Gideon wanted to take her in his arms. But it was too soon after the last disastrous time he'd done that, wasn't it? She had the sweetest smile though…

A cough behind him made him turn, startled.

The mayoress stood on the threshold, the local photographer behind him, grinning and with a large camera already raised to take snaps. Behind them came several other people, peering curiously through the windows at the floral displays in cream, gold and silver vases and urns, and the blown-up black and white photographs of Cecily on the wall. Some were elderly, and would have known Cecily personally, one white-haired lady exclaiming in delight as she pointed her walking stick at the framed photo of a young Cecily and Franklin that stood on the serving counter.

'Hello, Gideon,' the mayoress said with a meaningful smile. She was a tall, imposing woman in her forties, a few streaks of silver in her chestnut hair only making her look more distinguished. Today she was in half-regalia, chain about her neck but wearing a smart black-and-white checked suit instead of ceremonial robes. 'How are you?'

'Hello, Anna-May, very well, thank you,' he said smoothly, instantly in professional mode, shaking her hand. 'Good to see you. How are you?' When she murmured a smiling reply, he asked, 'And how are Pinky and Perky?'

'Chirpy as always,' she said with a genuine laugh, referring to her two middle-aged, yellow-plumed canaries. Her voice was proper Cornish, for her family had lived in these parts for generations, and indeed her husband ran a pig farm a few miles further inland, though the couple lived in town. 'I've been giving the little rascals a few strawberries and a handful of chopped melon every few days, like you suggested, and they're both much more active now, dear old things.'

'Glad to hear it. Though everything in moderation,' he reminded her.

'Oh, quite. We wouldn't want any nasty messes on the cage floor, would we?' The mayoress winked, and her gaze slid past him to Penny, who had been waiting patiently this whole time, hands clasped at her waist. 'And you must be Penny. I must say, you're younger than you sounded on the phone.'

The two women shook hands, though he saw how Penny winced slightly, her wide blue gaze shooting to his face. Why? What was wrong with her being younger than Anna-May had expected? Another mystery he would need to ask her about later, he expected. This was hardly the time.

'And you've transformed this old place... It was a shed after Cecily left. Cobwebs everywhere. Such a shame. But now, look at it!' Eagerly, Anna-May turned to the photographer. 'Lots of lovely shots of me with the new flower shop owner, Sam. They will look brilliant in the newspaper. And the county magazine too, if I have a word with the jolly old editor. He's an old friend of mine, did I say? Oh, I did? All right... Well, after this we'll get the grand reopening ribbon set up in the doorway for me to cut, and you can get some more lovely shots of that too. You have scissors?' she added, glancing sharply at Penny.

'Of course.'

'Excellent. Though I do always bring my own on these public occasions. Just in case... Best side, only, please, Sam.' And the mayoress tilted her head to the right while shaking Penny's hand firmly, the two women standing in front of the counter with its photograph of Cecily and Franklin, and rows of gorgeous-scented flowers in display vases rising in tiers behind them. 'Proper job!'

Penny smiled for the camera, but he could see how her gaze shifted occasionally to his face in the hour that followed, as the mayoress cut the grand reopening ribbon and officially declared, 'Our wonderful little flower shop is open again!' to a generous round of applause from all the townsfolk and well-wishers who had gathered to watch the ceremony. He could see she was anxious about something. But what?

Franklin turned up in good time too, with several nurses and other residents of the care home, and gasped in shock on seeing the flower shop as it had used to be.

He stood some time staring at the photos of Cecily, tears in his eyes. 'Beautiful,' the old gentleman kept muttering, tracing Cecily's face with a shaking finger, 'so beautiful. Oh, my dearest Cecily...' And then he would seem to tune out for a while, his gaze blurred as though back in the past, or perhaps turned inwards, forgetting where and even who he was, while the crowd buzzed about him, admiring the floral displays and scents.

Watching his godfather, Gideon could almost have cried himself.

CHAPTER ELEVEN

To Penny's relief, and trepidation too, they finally managed to find a time when both were free to walk along the stunning Merriweather promenade together – Sunday afternoon, since that was the only time the flower shop was closed now. They met at the war memorial and strolled along the front, side by side in the breezy Cornish sunshine, staring out at the ruffled blue-white Atlantic Ocean and making light, inconsequential conversation that came nowhere near ruffling the waves of their own hearts.

There were dozens of holiday-makers in shorts and swimsuits crammed onto the narrow strip of golden sand between rocky stretches, ignoring sharp gusts of wind, eating picnics, or attempting to play cricket or volleyball, with some intrepid souls even swimming against the oncoming tide.

Further out, the usual body-boarders and surfers in black wetsuits dotted the rolling waves, or fought against the current to swim beyond the breakers, though she knew these hardy types would be out in all weathers, not just on the sunnier days.

'I love Cornwall,' she said with a satisfied sigh.

'No doubts, then? No desire to go back home?' He looked at her sideways. 'What about your family back east?'

'My dad, you mean? And my stepmum, Sylvia?' She had told him various unappetizing tales of their antics during one of those late-night chats over wine. 'I'm afraid not. They have their own lives and I have mine. And never the twain shall meet. Oh, maybe at Christmas and birthdays and... and Father's Day etc.' She grimaced at baring her own dreadful inadequacies to him like this. Her character flaws. But she had never really been happy at home and he ought to know that about her. 'Does that make me a bad person?'

He gave a short laugh. 'No, it makes you one hundred percent normal.' Then his smile faded. 'So, you're planning to stay here?' he pressed her. 'To keep running the flower shop?'

'For now,' she said cautiously, wondering where his question was leaving.

He was silent for a moment, then said, 'People are still talking.'

'I know.'

'They don't know about you wanting to reenact Franklin and Cecily's dates.'

'I know.'

'So they think we're an item. That we're going out for real.' He paused, looking ahead. His dark hair blew about wildly in the gusty wind but he didn't smooth it down. 'That we're lovers.' His voice had deepened.

'I know,' she repeated, her tummy twisting in knots at that word.

Lovers.

Oh, if only, she was thinking fiercely, if only…

'And it just occurred to me,' he went on, still in that deep tone, still not looking at her, 'that if they're going to hang us for a sheep as much as a lamb, we might as well go down that path.'

She frowned, glancing about. 'Sorry? Which path?'

'This one,' he muttered, indicating a concrete slip road that led to the beach. A few chalet-style covered stalls had been set up on the slip road for the season, safe from the marauding sea – at least, so Penny hoped, noticing the white-topped waves rolling up the beach.

The fish and chip stall was open, its red and white-striped awning flapping in the wind, the smell of frying fish delicious, making her suddenly ravenous.

'Okay, yes,' she agreed.

They turned down onto the slip road, and she almost slipped on the striated surface, her old trainers not having much grip on the sole anymore. Though Gideon certainly had a grip on her soul, she thought dizzily. For his hand had shot out and caught her in an instant, keeping her upright with a steely strength.

'Thank you,' she gasped, very close to his face. And

his chest, she realised. And his muscular thighs in his faded blue denim jeans. Goodness, he was so damn sexy... 'I guess that's why they call this a slip road.'

He laughed.

'A sheep as much as a lamb,' she mumbled, struggling to think.

'An old country saying. It means –'

'No, I get it. That people would be hanged for a small theft as much as a big one, so you might as well go big.'

'Exactly.'

'But there was a path thing too...'

'Yes, I said we might as well go down there,' he explained, still not making much sense. Then she realised what he was alluding to. 'If people think we're involved, why not *really* get involved? Make things real between us, I mean,' he went on huskily, 'and start a proper relationship.' His dark gaze searched her face before he continued, and she wondered if he felt as uncertain as she did. 'We could do it, you know. I'd happily take that path. What do you think?'

Lovers.

'I think... I'm hungry.'

'Me too.' His body pressed against hers, his look intense.

'For chips,' she whispered.

He blinked, then released her. 'Yes, of course. Fish and chips on the prom. That was the deal, wasn't it?' He ran an impatient hair through his wind-tossed hair. 'Sorry.' His voice grated on the air, and she could see a sheen in his eyes. Was he upset? 'Yes, let's do this final thing for Cecily and Franklin. One last *homage*, as you put it.'

She stumbled on towards the fish and chip stall, blown by the Cornish sea breezes, the taste of salt on her lips. 'And vanilla ice cream after,' she almost groaned, wishing she knew what to do and say that wouldn't leave her in a deeply vulnerable position. She simply wasn't up for a brief fling with this man – he was a keeper, for sure, and she would want to be with him forever if they started sleeping together – and she feared that was all he was interested in. He'd never suggested otherwise, had he?

'I wonder if they do Rocky Road,' he muttered, right behind her.

'With sprinkles and chocolate sauce.'

'I'm right with you.' He took her hand, perhaps meaning that he wanted sprinkles too, perhaps that he would protect her if she fell again. 'All the way.'

'All the way,' she repeated, and could have screamed in frustration. Did this man even have a clue what he was doing to her? And when he said, 'We could take that path,' did he mean *forever*? Or just for a few sweet delirious weeks, for a Cornish summer fling…?

Gideon could have screamed in frustration. But he didn't want to startle her. Or make her think he'd stubbed a toe or maybe lost his mind. Though in truth he had lost his mind. And his heart too, it seemed. To this strange, nostalgic, heart-on-sleeve woman with the huge blue eyes whose stare did amazing things to his soul and whose generous curves did equally amazing things to his libido…

What the hell did he have to do to persuade her to start up a real relationship with him? He had tried kissing her – several times now, in fact, with varying degrees of success – and had tried suggesting they become lovers without being too blunt about it. And she was still resistant.

Yet he felt sure she was interested. More than interested. *Very* damn interested, if her shifting hips and audible gasps when he was kissing her were anything to go by. Unless he was so rusty at this gig, he'd started missing the signals that a woman was wriggling and gasping because she was trying to escape rather than get closer.

They bought a round of fish and chips each, and sat on a bench up on the prom to eat them, the paper rustling and flapping, but the smell entrancing.

'I haven't had fish and chips in ages,' he admitted, enjoying the delicious crunch of batter and the succulent cod flakes beneath. 'This cod tastes amazing. And the chips are perfect. Not too fat, not too thin, not too oily. And only a tiny dusting of salt for flavour.'

'Agreed,' Penny said, abandoning her wooden knife and fork to use her fingers. 'Mmm… Gorgeous!'

He watched her in covert amusement but continued to chase chips around himself with his own slightly accurate fork. Several people he knew had already walked by with a barely concealed grin and a wink. He didn't want to add disrepute to his Casanova public image by eating with his fingers. There were standards, after all…

Afterwards, they crossed the road to the ice cream parlour and sat there a while, chatting over tall sundaes liberally laced with chocolate sauce and nut sprinkles. She twirled her hair in her fingers, and leant her chin on her hand, and spoke nostalgically of her childhood while staring out at the sea. He was mesmerized and had no idea what he was saying in return to her remarks, only aware that he had fallen head over heels in love with this woman. He wished to goodness that he hadn't let her see those letters from Cecily to Franklin though, knowing how much they must have hurt her tender heart…

'I'm sorry,' he said abruptly, laying aside his sundae spoon.

She blinked and stared at him, surprised. 'About what?'

'Those letters… Having to learn about your mother's hard feelings towards your grandmother like that, and how she basically lied to you about Cecily, saying she was dead rather than let you get to know her.'

Colour crept into her cheeks. 'Oh, that.' Her head went down. 'Yes, that wasn't nice. I read those letters…' Her voice became muffled. 'But, you know, that was the past. We have to look to the future now. Do things differently.'

'Yes,' he agreed, watching her intently.

Stirring the last mushy leftovers of her ice cream sundae, she said indistinctly, 'Which is why we ought to... to be honest with each other.'

'Honest?'

Penny nodded. 'Tell the truth.'

'I didn't know I'd been lying to you.' He felt ruffled by the suggestion, his brows tugging sharply together.

'Not lying. But maybe not being completely *open*.'

Then Gideon understood. His breathing snagged in his chest and he pushed the tall sundae glass away with a jerk.

'About?'

'You know what about,' she said more clearly, and raised her head to glare at him. It was an accusing stare and it got under his skin.

'I'm glad you think so. I'm not sure I do,' he lied, suddenly on the defensive.

His heart was beating light and fast, and he felt cornered, like he needed to leap up from the table and escape. Which was ridiculous, wasn't it? Because he wanted this conversation to happen; he'd been longing to broach the topic himself for some days now, and had only held back out of delicacy, or possibly fear of what it might reveal.

He had tried to goad her into talking about their relationship earlier, in fact, before they'd stopped for fish and chips, and had been rebuffed. Now it was actually happening and he was behaving like a nervous schoolboy.

'Everything feels so stop-start. I... I like you,

Gideon.'

'You do?' He swallowed, and then sat back, trying to look nonchalant. 'Well, that's good to hear. Thank you, I suppose.'

'Don't be an ass.'

His gaze narrowed on her flushed face. 'I'm an ass now, am I?'

'Only because you're pretending not to understand what I'm saying. Anyway, I hadn't finished what I wanted to say. I like you,' she went on doggedly, 'but I don't know how you feel about me. And I'd like to.' She raised her brows at him, waiting.

'My turn, is it?'

'Speak now or forever hold your peace.'

If this blithe reference to the wedding ceremony was meant to rattle him, it did. He grimaced, even while his heart leapt at the suggestion. 'I like you too.'

'But *how much*?' She was pressuring him, her gaze locked with his. 'This much?' She drew a space between her two hands, and then doubled it. 'Or this much?' Then stretched her arms wide. 'Or even this much? Enough for a lifetime of "I like you's", perhaps?' She gave a little gasp as she added, 'Or only enough to last until the end of the summer, say?'

'You know how to needle a man.'

'I can't keep kissing you and not knowing what's behind it,' she hissed, leaning forward so nobody else in the ice cream parlour would hear.

'This is what's behind it,' he threw back at her, tapping his chest. 'Me.'

'But how much of you? And for how long?'

'All of me, damn you... And forever.' The words were out before he really knew what he was saying. Then he gulped and looked away, breathing hard. 'Satisfied?'

She said nothing for a space, staring back at him, wide-eyed, lips parted, her chest rising and falling rapidly as she digested the meaning behind those words.

Then she whispered, 'Yes.'

'Yes, what?' he demanded.

'Yes, I'm satisfied.' And she reached for his hand. 'I want you too, Gideon.'

Their eyes locked.

Five minutes later, the bill was paid and they were hurrying back along the promenade in the sunshine, the stunning view of the white-tipped Atlantic rollers forgotten, both intent on reaching his house or her flat as quickly as possible.

'My place or yours?' he asked as they reached the High Street.

'Your bed is bigger.' She blushed. 'I expect.'

'It is,' he agreed, and slipped an arm about her waist, loving the feel of her warm, pliant body, her hip bumping against his as they hurried. 'You're sure about this, Penny?'

'No, but I'm willing to give you the benefit of the doubt. Maybe you're a novice at this. But if you're even half as good in bed as you are at kissing, I'll take that and be grateful. We can always have a conversation about basics later.'

He gave a hoarse bark of laughter. 'You wretch... I assure you, I know what I'm doing in bed, you don't need to worry. I meant, are you sure you want to take a chance on me? On this relationship?' He paused. 'Because you've been holding back, I've felt it.'

'Only because you were holding back.'

'I was only holding back because you were holding back.'

'All right, whatever,' she whispered impatiently, and smiled at an old lady passing them in the street. As soon as the old lady was out of earshot, she went on, 'Chicken, egg... Let's just say we're both idiots and have done with it.'

'Agreed,' he whispered back, then jerked on her hand as they ran across the road. 'My place it is, then.'

A few weeks later, after she'd moved her possessions into Gideon's house, and they had settled into a lovely routine of eating breakfast together before going out to their respective workplaces every morning and then meeting again at the end of the day for dinner, a film or chat, followed by bed together, Penny already knew she'd made the right decision.

'Church wedding?' Gideon asked casually, glancing over his newspaper at her.

'Oh, I think so. Though we'll have to show willing by turning up to church a few times before asking the vicar.'

'I guess we can't escape that fate,' he said, but was

smiling.

Warmth and joy flooded her every time she thought of how wonderful he was as a lover, so kind and considerate, and yes, *nice*. But also fiery, heated, athletic…

All the good stuff.

And he could mend an animal's broken leg too.

But her real awareness that he was The One stemmed from that first evening when they'd slept together, after the walk on the prom and the fish and chips, and those long marvellous hours in bed, learning each other's bodies and sweet little proclivities…

After falling asleep blissfully in his arms at last, she had woken sometime in the early hours, startled by a voice whispering her name.

'Penny? Penelope, dearest?'

A familiar face had swum before her in the darkened bedroom, only a pale light showing from the landing through the partly open bedroom door…

'Ce-Cecily?' she'd whispered, slowly surfacing from sleep, sure she was still dreaming.

'I'm so glad you're happy, and that you've found love,' her grandmother's soft voice came into her head, and then a hand stroked her tousled hair. 'Embrace it, darling. Because this one's forever, I promise.'

Blinking, Penny had sat up, Gideon's arm falling away, and rubbed her sleepy eyes. 'Grandma? Is that really you?'

But the room had been dark and empty, no sign of Cecily anywhere.

'Hey, come back... Where did you go?' Gideon murmured, reaching gently for her. When she didn't say anything, he too sat up. 'What's the matter, sweetheart?' His voice was low and concerned. 'Bad dream?'

'No,' she'd said tremulously, still peering about the shadows in vain. It had started raining outside, she realised, the increasing pitter-patter of summer rain against the windows perhaps what she had heard in her sleep, what had woken her... Rainfall, not her grandmother's voice whispering to her from beyond the grave. 'Good dream. At least, I think so.'

'Come here. let me hold you.' Lovingly, they snuggled down under the covers, bare limbs tangling comfortably together. His hand stroked her hair back from her forehead, so tender and sensual, she felt her worries melt away at his touch. 'Ah... I love you so much, Penny.'

She turned to him, her eyes seeking his profile in the darkness. Her heart filled with so much emotion, she felt it start to leak from her eyes...

'I love you too, Gideon,' she replied, and heard him sigh with happiness.

And I love you too, Cecily, you wonderful grandmother, she thought gratefully into the darkness, smiling as her eyes closed and she drifted back to sleep in her husband-to-be's arms...

THE END

BOOKS BY THIS AUTHOR

The Oddest Little Cornish Christmas Shop

Artist Marjorie comes back to the tiny Cornish fishing village where she was born to take over the running of her ailing grandmother's Christmas shop, selling everything from Christmas trees to snowglobes to inflatable elves. The last person she expects to see back in the village for Christmas is her old adversary Jack, whose high-powered career has taken him all over the world. But Jack's sister is sick too, and he's come home to be with her...right next door!

Marjorie and Jack clashed back in the day, culminating in a kiss and a slapped face when they parted. Yet she's never got over his crooked smile and ironic one-liners. Can she handle his prickling proximity until her gran's better? Or is Marjorie in danger of making a fool of herself all over again?

Printed in Great Britain
by Amazon